"Am I being snubbed, Cressy?"

"Snubbed?" Cressida was so shocked at the idea, that she put a hand on Aldrik's arm. "How could I ever snub you? I don't know what I should have done without you."

She stared at him, suddenly and blindingly aware that she didn't know what she'd do without him. She said slowly, "I just don't think you need to be concerned about me any longer. I don't think I am explaining myself very well…."

"Then don't try," he advised her briskly. "Simply enjoy your new life and have a happy Christmas."

As he gave her a brightly wrapped box, she wished he would kiss her. But he didn't. He simply said goodbye and left.

Cressida lay awake for a good deal of that night. Love, she reflected, was by no means all it was cracked up to be.

Betty Neels is well-known for her romances set in the Netherlands, which is hardly surprising. She married a Dutchman and spent the first twelve years of their marriage living in Holland and working as a nurse. Today, she and her husband make their home in an ancient stone cottage in England's West Country, but they return to Holland often. She loves to explore tiny villages and tour privately owned homes there in order to lend an air of authenticity to the background of her books.

Books by Betty Neels

A HAPPY MEETING
Betty Neels

Harlequin Books

TORONTO • NEW YORK • LONDON
AMSTERDAM • PARIS • SYDNEY • HAMBURG
STOCKHOLM • ATHENS • TOKYO • MILAN
MADRID • WARSAW • BUDAPEST • AUCKLAND

Original hardcover edition published in 1992
by Mills & Boon Limited

ISBN 0-373-03267-6

Harlequin Romance first edition June 1993

A HAPPY MEETING

CHAPTER ONE

THE day had been warm for early October but now the sun was low on the horizon and there was a chilly breeze. The quiet country road running between the trees was full of shadows; in an hour or so it would be dusk. The girl sitting on the grass verge shivered a little and put her arm around the lean, unkempt animal beside her: a half-grown dog in a deplorable condition, the rope which had held him fast to a tree still dangling from his scraggy neck. It was when she had found him not an hour earlier and struggled to free him that he had knocked her down. She had fallen awkwardly and twisted her ankle, and getting herself as far as the road had been a nightmare that she was relieved to have done with. Now she sat, more or less patiently, hoping for help. Two cars had gone past since she had dragged herself and the dog to the road but although she had waved and shouted neither of them had stopped. She studied her ankle in the dimming light; it had swollen alarmingly and she hadn't been able to get her shoe off; there was nothing to do but wait for help, although, since the road was not much more than a country lane connecting two villages, there didn't seem much chance of that before early morning when the farm tractors would begin their work.

'We may have to spend the night,' she told the animal beside her, for the sound of her voice was a comfort of sorts, 'but I'll look after you, although I'm not sure how.' The animal cowered closer; she could feel its ribs against her side, and she gave it a soothing pat. 'It's nice to have company, anyway,' she assured him.

Dusk had fallen when she heard a car coming and presently its headlights swept over them as it passed.

'That's that,' said the girl. 'You can't blame anyone for not stopping...'

However, the car was coming back, reversing slowly until it was level with them and then stopping. The man who got out appeared to her nervous eyes to be a giant and she felt a distinct desire to get up and run, only she couldn't. He came towards her slowly and somehow when he spoke his voice was reassuringly quiet and calm.

'Can I help?' he asked, and his voice was kind too. 'You're hurt?'

He stood for a moment looking down at her; a small girl with no looks, too thin, but even in the deepening dusk her eyes were beautiful.

'Well, not really hurt, but I twisted my ankle and I can't walk.' She studied him carefully and liked what she saw. This was no young man out for an evening's ride but a soberly clad man past his first youth, his pale hair silvered at the temples. He was good-looking too, though that did not matter. 'I would be very grateful for a lift as far as Minton Cracknell; it's only a couple of miles along the road. I live there.'

'Of course, but may I look at your ankle first? I'm a doctor and it looks as though it needs attention.'

He squatted down beside her, and, when the dog growled, put out a large hand for the beast to sniff. 'We must have that shoe off,' he told her, and got out a pocket knife and cut the laces.

'I'm going to hurt you,' he said, and did despite his gentleness. 'Good girl. Catch your breath while I get some bandage from the car.'

He was gone and back again before she had had the time to wipe away the tears on her cheeks; she hadn't said a word while the shoe was coming off but she hadn't been able to stop the tears. He handed her a handkerchief without a word and said cheerfully, 'It will feel much better once I've strapped it up. You will have to get it X-rayed tomorrow and rest it for a day or two.'

He got to his feet. 'The dog is yours?' he asked.

'Well, no—I—I heard him barking as I came along the road and he'd been tied to a tree and left to starve; he accidentally tripped me up as I was freeing him...'

'Poor beast, but lucky for him that you heard him. Will you adopt him?'

He was talking idly, giving her time to pull herself together.

'Well, I don't think I can—my stepmother doesn't like dogs—but I can give him a bed and a meal and see if there's anyone in the village...'

'Well, let's get you home,' he said kindly, and scooped her up with a word to the dog, who needed no encouragement but climbed into the back of the car after the girl had been settled in the front seat.

'He'll make an awful mess,' she said apologetically, 'and it's a Bentley, isn't it?'

The man looked amused. 'I don't suppose there will be any lasting damage,' he observed. 'Where do you live exactly?'

'If you go through the village it's the house on the right behind a high brick wall. It's called the Old Rectory. My father inherited it from his father; it's been in the family for years...'

She glanced at his profile. 'You've been very kind.'

'I'm glad that I happened to pass by, Miss...?'

'Preece, Cressida Preece.' She added shyly, 'You're not English, are you?'

'Dutch. Van der Linus—Aldrik van der Linus.'

She said politely, 'Your English is quite perfect. Oh, here's the village.'

The narrow main street of the little place was empty; it was the hour of high tea and lights shone from windows as they passed the small houses lining it.

'It's just along here, past the church...'

The houses had petered out and the car's lights touched on the brick wall and an open gate. The drive was short, ending in a small sweep before a nice old house, not over large but solidly built. The man got out but before he reached the door it was opened by a severe-looking woman with iron-grey hair drawn back into a bun. She had a long thin face and sharp, very dark eyes, and she was dressed in a shabby dress under a white apron.

She looked at the man with a belligerence which he ignored.

'I have brought Miss Preece home,' he told her. 'She has damaged her ankle. If you will tell me where her room is, I will carry her indoors. I think there is no lasting damage but she should rest it for a few days.'

The woman didn't answer him but brushed past him and out to the car.

'Miss Cressida, what has happened? Are you hurt? You must get to your bed...'

The girl spoke matter-of-factly, 'Moggy, dear, I'm quite all right, just sprained an ankle. Mother's not back?' There was a hint of anxiety in her voice, and the man, who had come to stand by the car, frowned.

'No, thank the lord. We'll get you indoors.' Moggy heard a faint growl from the back seat and exclaimed 'What's that—an animal...?'

'A dog, Moggy. I found him tied to a tree. We'll have to hide him tonight and tomorrow I'll go to the village and try and find a home for him.' Cressida undid her seatbelt. 'He must have a meal, he's starved.'

'She'll not allow it. We'll get you to your room and I'll feed him and take him down to old Mr Fellows and ask if he will keep the beast in his shed...'

'It might be advisable to get Miss Preece up to her bed,' said the man gently, 'and since I gather the dog is not welcome here I'll take him with me. I'm going in to Yeovil; there's a good vet there.'

'A vet?' said Cressida sharply. 'He's not to be put to sleep...'

'Certainly not. And now, if I may, I'll carry you indoors and perhaps when we have you settled this animal might be given a small meal.' And at her look of doubt, 'I give you my word that he'll be properly looked after.' He had spoken quietly but Moggy stood back without a word and allowed him to lift Cressida from the car and carry her into the house.

'Up the stairs,' she told him gruffly, 'and down that passage beyond the landing.'

He went up the wide oak staircase unhurriedly, carrying Cressida with no effort, and waited while Moggy went ahead of them and opened a door at the end of the passage.

The room was small and plainly furnished and Dr Van der Linus frowned again, for it seemed to him that it was a room suitable to a servant, not the daughter of the house. He laid her gently on the bed and stooped to take a look at the ankle.

'I suggest that you take a couple of paracetamol before you settle for the night,' he observed, 'and be sure and get your doctor to come and look at it in the morning.

He may wish to re-strap it and give you instructions as to treatment. You will need to keep off your feet for a few days but he will do what is necessary.' He stood looking down at her. 'Have you paracetamol? Take two as soon as possible with a drink.'

He took her hand in his large one. 'A most unfortunate accident, but you will be quite all right again very shortly. And don't worry about the dog, I'll see that it comes to no harm. Goodbye, Miss Preece.'

She didn't want him to go; a sensible girl, inured to accepting what life had to offer her, she wished very much that he would stay. But that, of course, was impossible; he was a complete stranger who had happened to turn up just when he was most needed. Then she thanked him in a polite voice tight with pain and watched his vast back go through the door with regret. At least the dog would be safe and her stepmother had been away from home. She comforted herself with that.

Dr van der Linus trod slowly down the staircase with Moggy leading the way. In the hall he stood still. 'You will look after Miss Preece? She is in a good deal of pain, but get her into bed with a warm drink and the paracetamol and she should sleep. Her own doctor will prescribe what he thinks fit.' He smiled down at the severe face. 'Could I bother you for some water for the dog, and perhaps a slice of bread?' And at her nod, 'May I know your name?'

'Mogford—Miss, but Miss Cressy always calls me Moggy, since she was knee-high.' She went ahead of him. 'I've some soup on the stove; perhaps a drop of that would do the beast some good, then I'll go and see to Miss Cressy.'

She led the way into the kitchen and poured soup into a bowl and broke some bread into it. 'You won't be

long?' she asked anxiously. 'Mrs Preece doesn't hold with
animals. It's a mercy that she's out . . . there'll be a fuss
enough over Miss Cressy.'

'Yes. I'm sure your mistress will be upset,' observed
Dr van der Linus smoothly.

'Upset? Oh, she'll be upset, all right.' She glanced at
the clock. 'She'll be back in twenty minutes or so, you'd
best hurry.'

Dr van der Linus's eyebrows rose but all he said was,
'I'll be very quick. Shall I leave the bowl behind a bush
for you to collect later?'

His companion nodded. 'Thank you for your trouble.
You've been most kind.'

She shut the front door upon him and he went to the
car, let the dog out while it ate and drank hungrily and
then ushered it back in. He had driven a couple of miles
and was almost at Templecombe when a car flashed past
him. There was a woman driving. Probably Mrs Preece,
he reflected as he turned off the road to take the short
cut to Yeovil and the vet.

That gentleman, roused from his comfortable chair
by the fire, peered at the dog standing dejectedly on the
end of its rope. 'My dear Aldrik, what on earth have
you here?'

'A dog, John. I have acquired him from his rescuer
who is unable to offer food and shelter. Found tied to
a tree on the other side of Minton Cracknell.'

'Want me to have a look? He's in pretty poor shape.'
He patted the dog's matted head. 'I didn't know you
were over here. Staying with Lady Merrill? You must
come and dine one evening before you go back.'

He led the way through the house and out again into
a yard at the back to his surgery. 'How is the old lady?'

'In splendid form. Her years sit lightly on her.' He heaved the reluctant dog on to the examination table, gentling him with a steady hand.

'Over here on holiday or doing some work?'

'Oh, a little of both. I've had a week in Edinburgh; I'm going on to Bristol to give a series of lectures and then back to London before I go home.'

'Well, dine with us before you leave. Molly will be disappointed if you don't. How about one evening next week? Any evening, take pot luck.'

'I should like that. May I give you a ring?'

The vet was bending over the dog. 'He hasn't anything broken as far as I can see. Half starved—more than half—and ill-treated—look at these sores. Do you want me to get him fit, or...?'

'Get him fit, will you? I promised his rescuer; a dab of a girl with huge brown eyes.'

John looked up. 'You say he was found near Minton Cracknell? That would be Cressida Preece. She brought me a cat a month or two ago—in a bad way, paid to have her cured of burns, quite nasty ones as a result of some lout tying a squib to her tail. She's still paying me, a bit at a time.'

'And yet she lives in a pleasant house...?'

'Yes but I fancy her life isn't as pleasant. Her father died some months ago; she lives with her stepmother. Unfortunately he left everything to her under the impression, one presumes, that she would provide for his daughter.'

Dr van der Linus stroked the trembling dog's head. 'Surely in this day and age the girl can leave home and get a job?'

'One would think so, though I don't imagine she's trained for anything. What shall I do? Get this beast fit and let her know?'

'No. I've taken rather a fancy to him. I'll take him with me when I go back to Holland. May I leave him with you? My grandmother will be wondering where I have got to.'

'Give me a ring in the morning, and we'll see how he is after some food and a night's sleep.'

The doctor got back into his car and drove away from the town, going north and presently turning into a maze of side-roads which brought him eventually to a small village lying between hilly country. It was indeed a small place, with a church, a handful of cottages, and a handsome vicarage, a shop and a duck pond. He drove through it before turning in between red-brick pillars surmounted by weatherbeaten lions and following a drive between thick undergrowth. It ended in a wide gravel sweep before a red-brick house of the Queen Anne period, light streaming from its windows and ringed around by trees. Dr van der Linus, getting out of his car, thought how welcoming it was. The door was opened as he reached it and a dignified old man, rather shaky on his legs, wished him a good evening and offered the information that Lady Merrill was in the small drawing-room.

'I'm late, Baxter—I got held up. Give me ten minutes before you serve dinner, will you?' He clapped the old man gently on the shoulders and crossed the hall to one of the open doors.

The room was a pleasant one, a little old-fashioned but light and airy with some rather massive furniture and thickly carpeted. The doctor crossed to a chair by the fire and the old lady sitting in it turned a smiling face to him as two Pekinese dogs hurried to meet him. He bent to pat them before stooping to kiss his grandmother.

'My apologies for being late, my dear. I was unexpectedly delayed.'

'Did the lecture not go well?'

'Oh, very well. I was forced to stop on my way...'

'Pour yourself a drink and tell me about it.'

Which he did. 'Was she pretty, this girl?'

'Pretty? To tell you the truth, I can't remember how she looked. She had nice eyes and a very pleasant voice.' He sounded indifferent and presently they talked of other things. He didn't think of the girl again.

Cressida, with Miss Mogford's help, had got herself into bed. Her ankle hurt abominably but the paracetamol was beginning to take effect. Moggy had arranged a small footstool in the bed so that her foot was free of the bedclothes and perhaps by the morning it would be better. Staying in bed was a luxury her stepmother disapproved of. Hopefully she wouldn't come home until late and need know nothing about it until the morning. She drank the tea Miss Mogford brought her and was urged to go to sleep, and she did as she was bid. She was awakened half an hour later by the entrance of Mrs Preece, a woman who in her youth had been enchantingly pretty and now in middle age, by dint of dieting ruthlessly, going to the best hairdressers so that her once golden hair should show no hint of grey, using every aid to beauty which caught her eye in the glossy magazines she favoured and wearing the floating draperies which gave her the look of helpless femininity which hid a nature as cold and hard as steel, preserved the illusion of sweetness of character.

'What is all this nonsense I hear from Miss Mogford?' she wanted to know. 'And why are you in bed? It's barely nine o'clock? Really, Cressida, I hardly expect a healthy girl of four and twenty to loll around like this.'

Cressida, used to her stepmother's manner towards her, sat up in bed. 'I'm in bed because I can't stand on my foot and it's very painful. I dare say it will be all right by the morning.'

'It had better be—I've the Worthingtons coming to dinner and I want the flowers done and the silver epergne properly polished.' She sighed heavily. 'I've a splitting headache; I was forced to come away early from the party. I shall go to bed and can only hope that Miss Mogford will spare the time to bring me a hot drink and run my bath.'

She went away without saying goodnight and Cressida wriggled down into her bed again, wide awake now and aware that her ankle was hurting. It was too soon to take any more paracetamol. She tugged her pillows into comfort and allowed her thoughts to roam.

The man who had brought her home had been nice; not just nice, he had treated her...she sought for words— as though she mattered; and since she knew only too well that her looks were negligible she had appreciated that. He had been surprised when he'd seen her room, she had noticed that at once, but since she wasn't going to see him again she didn't think that mattered. She knew that the few friends she had in the village were at a loss to understand why she stayed at home when it was so obvious that she wasn't welcome there now that her father was dead. She had never told anyone that she stayed there because of Moggy. Moggy had no home of her own; she had worked all her life for Cressida's parents, never able to save because she had a married

sister whose husband had become paralysed soon after
they had married and had lived for many years, a helpless
wreck, his life made bearable by the extras Moggy's
earnings had helped to buy. Now at fifty-eight years, she
had two more years before she could draw her pension
and receive the annuity Mr Preece had left her. Until
then there was nothing else she could do but stay with
Mrs Preece, since that lady had led her to understand
that unless she remained in her employ until her sixtieth
birthday her annuity would be cancelled. Since Miss
Mogford, for all her severe appearance, was afraid that
no one else would employ her in any case, and, over and
above that, had set her heart on going to live with her
now widowed sister where she would enjoy a snug retirement, she stayed on, managing the house with the
help of girls from the village and Cressida. It was only
because Cressida understood Moggy's situation that she
stayed. Two years, she told herself repeatedly, would
soon pass, and once Moggy was safely esconced with
her sister she herself would feel free to go away. She had
no idea what she would do, she hadn't been trained for
anything but she was handy about the house and even
in this day and age there were old ladies who needed
companions. A roof over her head and some money to
spend was all she expected until she had found her feet.

It was a great pity that her father, that most trusting
of men, had left everything to her stepmother, under the
impression that she would give Cressida an allowance.
Instead of that, Mrs Preece had lost no time in making
it quite clear that that was out of the question. Cressida
would have to help Miss Mogford and in return she
would be clothed and fed and be given pocket money.

Cressida, after a number of indignant protests, had
had every intention of leaving, only to be stymied by

being told of Moggy's situation. She had plenty of common sense, added to which she was a girl of spirit, but Moggy had been a faithful and loving employee and a pleasant retirement was almost within her grasp. Cressida stayed and those who knew her thought silently that she should have shown more spirit.

She confided in no one, even her closest friends, and since Mrs Preece was always charmingly maternal towards her when there was anyone around they began to think that Cressida liked the way she lived. She was always cheerful and showed no envy when friends became engaged or got themselves good jobs away from the village, and they weren't to know of the long hours she spent planning her future. She didn't brood, for she despised self-pity, but now and then she wished that she had even a modicum of good looks; a pretty face, she was sure, would be a great help in getting a job.

She dozed off, to wake in the night from the throbbing of her ankle.

Moggy came to see how she was in the morning, took one look at her white face and told her to stay where she was.

'I can't,' said Cressida, 'there are the flowers to arrange and some silver to polish.' So saying she got out of bed, set her injured foot floor and did something she had never done before in her life. She fainted.

Moggy picked her up and put her on the bed and marched down to Mrs Preece's bedroom. Regardless of the fact that it was still two hours short of her usual entry with a tray of tea, she roused her mistress briskly.

'Miss Cressida's fainted, on account of her trying to get up because you told her to,' said Miss Mogford with a snap. 'You'd best get the doctor to her.'

Mrs Preece sat up in bed. 'For a sprained ankle? Probably she's only wrenched it badly. Certainly not, but I suppose she'd better stay in bed for the time being. What a nuisance this is and now I shall have a headache being wakened so abruptly. Really, you might consider my nerves.'

She sank back on her pillows. 'Go away and bring my tea at the usual time.'

Miss Mogford went away, muttering darkly to herself once the door was shut. Things couldn't go on like this; something would have to be done, although she had no idea what it was. She went to the kitchen and made a pot of tea and bore it upstairs to Cressida's room and shared it with her. It was hot and strong, and, lulled by the paracetamol, Cressida felt better.

'I could get up,' she suggested, 'if I had a stick...'

'Nonsense, you'll do no such thing. That nice doctor who brought you home would be very annoyed if he knew.'

'He doesn't know,' said Cressida, and felt a pang of regret because of that. She was a sensible girl, concealing a romantic nature beneath her ordinary appearance; no good would come of wanting something she couldn't have. She contrived to wash with Moggy's aid, brushed her hair, which was long and mousy, and plaited it and set about persuading Moggy to bring the silver epergne upstairs. 'With an old newspaper,' she urged, 'and the polish and cloths. I can do it easily and it will keep me occupied.'

'All right,' Moggy was grudging, 'but only when you've had your breakfast.'

'I'm not hungry...'

'You'll eat what I bring you,' said Moggy.

*   *   *

Dr van der Linus was up early, to walk in the garden with the dogs and enjoy the crisp sunshine of the morning. He had slept soundly but he was aware of uneasiness; although he could barely remember what the girl he had helped on the previous evening looked like, he was unable to shake off the feeling that he ought to do something about her. He hadn't liked the vague air of disquiet which she and the woman who admitted them had had and he had been puzzled at the bare little room which was surely unsuitable for a daughter of the house. The housekeeper had been anxious for him to leave, too.

He went indoors to his breakfast. It might be a good idea to get the name of the local doctor and give him a ring; on the other hand, that smacked of officiousness. He sighed and poured himself some more coffee. It would be better if he were to call and enquire. He was to lunch with friends at Castle Cary and need not go much out of his way.

He went upstairs to his grandmother's room presently. She was sitting up in bed, her breakfast on a tray before her.

'Come in and finish this toast,' she begged him. 'Mrs Wiffin has this passion for feeding me up! Aren't you going over to Castle Cary to the Colliers'? Is Jenny at home?'

He smiled slowly. 'Matchmaking, Grandmother? I don't know if she's at home. In any case...' He paused. 'It is time I married, but not Jenny.'

'You've found the girl?' asked Lady Merrill eagerly.

'I'm not sure. She's very suitable. Her name is Nicola van Germert—you've met her. The daughter of one of the professors at Leiden University. We know all the same people and share a similar lifestyle.'

Lady Merrill bit into her toast. 'Not good reasons for marriage, my dear, but you're old enough and wise enough to know what you want. Most men want love as well,' she added drily.

He got up. 'Well, I suppose we aren't all lucky enough to find it. Will you be at home at teatime? We can sit in the garden, if it's warm enough, and gossip.' He bent to kiss her cheek. 'Staying here with you is something I always look forward to.'

'So do I, my dear. But you would be lost without your work. Don't you miss the hospitals and clinics and patients?'

'Oh, yes, very much. They are the most important things in my life, Grandmother.'

'Part of your life, Aldrik. Now run along and enjoy yourself.'

At the door he turned. 'I thought I'd call in on my way and see how that girl is getting on. I must find out about the dog too and let her know.'

'That would be kind.' Lady Merrill watched his vast back disappear through her door. She looked thoughtful. Considering the girl was so uninteresting that he couldn't remember what she looked like Aldrik was being very kind. But, of course, he was a kind man.

He drove away in the Bentley presently. Minton Cracknell wasn't all that distance away but there was no direct road to it. He needed to go considerably out of his way to reach it but since it was less than ten miles to Castle Cary from there and for most of the way a main road he would have time to make his call.

The house looked pleasant enough as he got out of the car but the housekeeper's face bore a look of gloomy indignation. The doctor was used to dealing with every

kind of person; his 'good morning' was briskly friendly
with strong overtones of authority.

'I've called to enquire after Miss Preece. I'm on my
way to friends and had to pass the door.'

'She's in bed but that ankle's that swollen, I don't like
the look of it...'

'The doctor is calling?'

She shook her head, speaking softly. 'Mrs Preece says
it's not necessary.'

'Perhaps I might have a word with her? I know it isn't
my business but perhaps I might persuade her.'

Miss Mogford's stern visage crumpled. 'Oh, sir, if you
would. I don't know what to do...'

She stood aside to allow him to enter and left him in
the hall while she went to find Mrs Preece.

She came back presently. 'If you'd come this way,
sir...'

Mrs Preece was sitting by a briskly burning fire, a tray
of coffee beside her, and she didn't get out of her chair.

'You must forgive me for not getting up,' she said in
a small plaintive voice. 'I'm not very strong. I understand that you were so kind as to bring Cressida home
yesterday. Do sit down—it is most kind of you to call
too.' She said sharply to Miss Mogford hovering at the
door, 'Bring some more coffee, will you? This is cold...'

The doctor sat, accepted the coffee when it came,
listened with apparent sympathy to his hostess's light
voice describing various aspects of her ill health, put
down his cup and said in a gentle voice, 'I should like
to see your stepdaughter's ankle; just to check on the
strapping. She will be going for an X-ray some time
today, I expect?'

Mrs Preece gave a tinkling laugh. 'Good heavens, no,
Doctor, it's only a sprain. She should be up and about

in no time. So vexing that she should have to stay in bed but she has never fainted before, the silly girl. And I have guests for dinner this evening too.'

'But you have no objection to my seeing her?' asked the doctor, and something in his voice made her shrug her shoulders and give a reluctant consent.

'Do encourage her to get up—she will be much better on her feet, will she not?' Mrs Preece gave him a charming smile, her head a little on one side. Really, she thought, he was so good-looking and charming that one would agree to anything that he might say.

'No, she would be much worse,' said Dr van der Linus. He spoke with such calm charm that she didn't realise that he had contradicted her flatly.

'Well, Miss Mogford shall take you to her room,' said Mrs Preece, 'I find the stairs trying—I have to be careful.'

She sounded wistful and long-suffering and if she expected the doctor to enquire sympathetically as to the reason she was to be disappointed.

Miss Mogford, summoned, led him up the stairs in silence. Only at Cressida's door she paused to look at him. She still said nothing, though she tapped on the door and opened it for him to go into the room.

Cressida was sitting up in bed, her small person surrounded by sheets of newspaper upon which rested the silver epergne which she was polishing. There was nothing beautiful about her; her hair hung in its long plait over one shoulder, her face, un-made-up, shone with her exertions, and she had a smear on one cheek and both hands were grimed with silver polish. The doctor, a kind man, eyed her with much the same feelings which he would have displayed if he had encountered a kitten or a puppy in need of help.

His, 'Good morning, Miss Preece,' was uttered with impersonal courtesy, and, since she was staring at him, open-mouthed, he said, 'I happened to be passing and felt that the least I could do was to enquire about your ankle.'

Cressida shut her mouth with a snap. She said politely, 'How kind of you. I'm fine, thank you.' She gave him a small smile. 'Isn't it a lovely morning?'

'Splendid. May I look at your ankle? It is of course, none of my business, but I feel that it should be X-rayed.'

'Well, I'm not sure,' began Cressida, to be told by Moggy to hush.

'The doctor knows best,' said that lady sternly. 'Just you lie still, Miss Cressida, and let him take a look.'

The doctor bent his great height and examined the ankle. When he had looked his fill he straightened up again. 'I'm not your doctor so I can do very little to help you, but I will do my best to advise your step-mother to allow the doctor to see you. It is a nasty sprain. It will get better quickly enough, though, provided it receives the right treatment.'

'And if it doesn't?' asked Cressida in a matter-of-fact voice.

'You will hobble around for a long time—a painful time too.'

'Well, thank you. It was very kind of you to come. I suppose you don't know what happened to that poor dog?'

'He needs only good food and rest and good care.' He smiled down at her. 'I shall take him back with me when I go to Holland.'

Her ordinary face was transformed by delight. 'Oh, how absolutely super! I'm sure he'll be a very handsome beast when he's fully grown.'

The doctor concealed his doubts admirably. 'I have no doubt of that.'

He put out a hand and engulfed hers in its firm grasp.

'You'll have to wash your hand,' said Cressida in her sensible way, 'it's covered in polish.' And then she added, 'I hope you have a good journey home.'

After he had gone she sat in her bed, the epergne forgotten, feeling lonely and somehow bereft.

Beyond registering his opinion that Cressida should have her ankle X-rayed, the doctor didn't waste time with Mrs Preece. He pleaded an urgent engagement and drove away.

In the village he stopped, enquired as to where the doctor lived and presented himself at the surgery door. Dr Braddock was on the point of leaving on his rounds.

'Van der Linus...' he said. 'I know that name. You wrote an article in the *Lancet* last month about neutropenia—a most interesting theory. Come in, come in, I'm delighted to meet you.'

'I've been poaching on your preserves,' said Dr van der Linus. 'If I might explain...'

Dr Braddock heard him out. 'I'll go this morning. I know—we all know—that things aren't right at the Old Rectory. Little Cressida is a dear child but one cannot interfere—though I will do my best to get her into hospital for a few days for she will never be able to get the proper rest she needs if she is at home...'

'It puts me in mind of Cinderella and her stepmother,' observed Dr van der Linus.

Dr Braddock nodded. 'Ridiculous, isn't it, in this day and age? There is obviously some reason which is keeping Cressida at home but she isn't going to tell anyone what it is.'

Dr van der Linus went on his way presently; he was going to be late for lunch at the Colliers'. As indeed he was, but he was an old friend and readily forgiven and moreover Jenny was an amusing companion. He told himself that he had done all that he could for Cressida Preece; she was a grown woman and should be capable of arranging her own life.

On his way back to his grandmother's house he reflected that she had seemed quite content with her lot. Probably things would improve. He frowned, aware that he was finding it difficult to forget her. 'Which is absurd,' he muttered. 'I can't even remember what she looks like.'

CHAPTER TWO

CRESSIDA, putting a final polish on the table silver, was astonished when Moggy opened the door to admit Dr Braddock.

He wished them a good morning, patted her on the shoulder and signified his intention of examining her ankle.

'However did you know about it?' asked Cressida and tried not to wince as he prodded it gently.

'Dr van der Linus very correctly informed me. How fortunate that he should have found you, my dear. I couldn't better the strapping myself but you must have it X-rayed. I've got my car outside. I'll run you in to Yeovil now and get it done...'

'Must you? I mean, Stepmother's got a dinner party this evening...'

'There is no need for her to come with you,' said Dr Braddock testily. He turned to Miss Mogford. 'Do you suppose we could give her a chair downstairs? Just get her into a dressing-gown.'

'How shall I get back here?' asked Cressida sensibly.

'Well, I have to come home, don't I?' He went to the door. 'I'll go and see your stepmother while Miss Mogford gets you ready, and don't waste time.'

'The silver,' said Cressida urgently, watching Moggy bundling it up, 'I haven't quite finished it.'

'Pooh,' said Miss Mogford, 'that's of no importance. Here's your dressing-gown.'

Doctor Braddock came back presently and between them he and Miss Mogford carried Cressida down to the hall and out of the door, into his car. Mrs Preece came after them, on the verge of tears. 'What am I to do?' she asked pathetically. 'There's the table to arrange and the drinks and the flowers to do. Really, Cressida, I do think you're being very selfish...'

No one answered her. The doctor and Moggy were too occupied in conveying Cressida as painlessly as possible and Cressida was gritting her teeth against the pain.

Dr Braddock drove off and as soon as she had control of her voice again she asked, 'They won't keep me long? I really should get back to help as quickly as I can. If I could be back by lunchtime? You're awfully kind having given me a lift, Dr Braddock, but I expect you have to come back home for lunch.'

She wasn't back for lunch, however; instead she found herself in one of the side-wards, comfortably in bed with a cradle over the injured ankle and the prospect of several days' rest.

'I really can't,' she explained to the cheerful house doctor who came to see her after she was warded. 'I haven't anything with me and there is a great deal I must do at home...'

'Well, if you don't rest that foot for a few days you won't be doing anything at all at home or anywhere else. Dr Braddock is going to call and see your stepmother on his way home. I dare say she will come and see you and bring you anything you need.'

The very last thing that lady would do, but there was no point in saying so. Cressida murmured suitably and since the bed was comfortable and she had had an irksome morning she closed her eyes and took a nap.

Miss Mogford came that evening, carrying a small holdall with what she considered necessary for Cressida's comfort while she was in hospital.

Cressida was delighted to see her, but worried too. 'Moggy, however did you get away? It's the dinner party too...is Stepmother very cross?'

'Livid,' said Miss Mogford, succinctly, 'but Dr Braddock was quite sharp with her, told her she was responsible for you and I don't know what else—I just happened to be passing through the hall and the door wasn't quite closed—so when he'd gone she phoned a catering firm and they're there now, seeing to everything. She told me to bring you what you needed here and I got the baker's van to bring me.'

'How will you get back?'

'The van's going back in an hour—the driver's got the day off tomorrow.'

'I don't know how long I'm here for...'

'I heard Dr Braddock say a couple of days, so you have a nice rest, Miss Cressida, and you'll have to take things easy when you come home.'

'Is my stepmother very annoyed?'

'Well, she's put out,' said Miss Mogford, uttering the understatement of a lifetime.

It was surprising what two days at the hospital did for Cressida. Of course there were the painful physiotherapy sessions, but for a good deal of each day she sat, the injured ankle resting on a stool, reading the discarded magazines and newspapers of the other patients, racing through the romantic fiction the lady from the hospital library was kind enough to bring her. She didn't turn up her unassuming nose at the food either; by the end of the second day she had colour in her cheeks and had put on a much-needed pound or two.

It was after breakfast on the following morning that the orthopaedic registrar came to tell her that she was fit enough to go home. 'You must wear an elastic stocking for a couple of weeks and keep off your feet as much as possible, and mind you rest the ankle properly. Sister phoned your stepmother and she assures us that you will be well looked after. We'll arrange for the hospital car service to pick you up after midday dinner today.'

Cressida thanked him and reflected that with a stocking and a stick she would be able to manage well enough. Indeed, she would have to...

She was sitting dressed and ready to leave, her ankle resting on the stool before her, when the door opened and Dr van der Linus walked in.

His greeting was genial. 'I had to have a word with someone here and thought I would call and see how you are getting on. I hear you're going home?'

'Yes. I'm waiting for transport. I'm quite better again.' She gave him a steady smile. 'I'm most grateful for everything you did for me.'

'Think nothing of it. I'm going past your home; I'll take you if you're ready to go. Just let me have a word with Sister...' He had gone before she could answer.

On the way back he told her that he was going to London on the following day and then back to Holland. 'I don't expect to be back here for some time,' he told her, and then casually, 'Have you any plans for your future?'

'No, none,' said Cressida bleakly. Her look was sad. 'At least not for some time.'

'Ah, well,' said the doctor easily, 'I dare say you have your reasons for staying at home.'

'Yes, I have. What will happen to the dog while you're in London?'

He accepted the change of subject without demur. 'He's to stay at the vet's. I will collect him when I leave England. He looks quite handsome, you know, although I'm not quite sure what he is. He's young still, about six months, and still going to grow.'

'You'll have room for him at your home?'

'Oh, yes.' He stopped in front of her house and got out to help her.

'Thank you very much,' she said. 'Would you like to come in and see my stepmother?'

The doctor smiled a little; it was obvious that she hoped that he would refuse. 'Why not?' he said cheerfully, and took her arm. 'Use your stick,' he counselled her, and, 'Put your weight on your good foot and for heaven's sake don't stand about; sit when you can and keep your foot up.'

Miss Mogford had been on the watch for Cressida's return. She opened the door wide, and her severe features softened into a smile. 'There, that's better. My goodness, a couple of days in hospital have done you a power of good, Miss Cressy—I swear you've put on a pound or two.'

'Is my stepmother in?' asked Cressida. 'I'm sure Dr van der Linus——'

The rest of her words were lost in Mrs Preece's voice, 'Is that you, Cressida? And about time too. All this rubbish I've been hearing about this ankle of yours...' A half-open door was thrust open and she came into the hall, caught sight of the doctor's vast person and went on smoothly, 'You poor child, have you had a lot of pain? I didn't come to visit you for you know how sensitive I am about illness.' She smiled at Dr van der Linus.

'My nerves, you know—I'm a martyr to them.' She turned to Cressida. 'Run along upstairs, dear, I dare say you would like a rest. Miss Mogford shall bring you your tea presently.'

She turned her back on Cressida, 'Tea is just made,' she said to the doctor. 'Do have a cup with me. I see so few people and you must tell me about Cressida's ankle.'

He refused with a charm as smooth as her own. 'I have an evening appointment and have still some distance to drive. Miss Preece should be all right now—a week or two keeping off the ankle and plenty of rest. But, of course, you will know what to do.'

He shook hands again and then turned to Cressida standing so quietly close by. 'I am sure that Dr Braddock will be over to see you shortly. I'm glad that the damage wasn't worse. I'll take care of the dog.'

She smiled. 'I'm sure you will and it's very kind of you to have him. I hope you have a good journey home.'

He stared down at her—such a plain little face but such beautiful eyes, and despite her smile she was unhappy. Not surprisingly, he considered; he had a poor view of Mrs Preece.

Sitting opposite his grandmother that evening, he voiced his vague disquiet about Cressida. 'The girl seems sensible enough,' he observed, 'and really one hardly expects the modern young woman to behave like Cinderella. Mrs Preece is someone that anyone with an ounce of good sense would get away from as quickly as possible.'

'Then there must be a good reason for the girl to remain there. Have you any idea what it might be?'

'None.' He added, 'I suppose there is no way of finding out?'

'Well, of course there is; ask her.'

'Perhaps I will. I must go up to town tomorrow but I'll come down to say goodbye before I go over to Holland, my dear, and I'll make time to see her then.' He frowned. 'Do you think I'm making a mountain out of a molehill? Probably I shall get short shrift...'

'In that case you need do no more about it. On the other hand she may be longing to confide in someone.'

It was a week later when he came back to Lady Merrill's and on a sudden impulse turned off the main road to go to Minton Cracknell. He was within half a mile of the village when he saw Cressida, walking awkwardly with a stick, going in the same direction as he was. He drew up beside her, and opened the door. His 'Hello, can I give you a lift?' was casually uttered and when she turned to look at him he was careful to stay casual. She had been crying, although she smiled now and thanked him politely.

'That's kind of you, but I walk a little way each day, you know—it's good for me.'

The doctor said, 'Get in, Cressida,' in a gentle voice which none the less she felt compelled to obey. She got in.

'Is your stepmother at home?'

She shook her head. 'No. She goes to Bath to have her hair done. Did you want to see her?'

'No. Why have you been crying, Cressida?' He leaned across her and closed the door. 'Supposing you tell me what is wrong? And I must beg you not to tell me that there is nothing wrong, because that is merely wasting time. Possibly you do not wish to confide in a friend but since we are unlikely to meet again you can safely unburden yourself to me.'

'I don't think,' began Cressida doubtfully, 'actually, that it would be of any interest to you.'

'You are politely telling me that it is none of my
business. Quite right, and all the more reason to talk to
me. Since it is none of my business I shall give you no
advice, nor shall I read you a lecture or tell you that
none of it matters.' He laid a great arm along the seat
behind her shoulders. 'Now let's have it...'

It was hard to start, it had been all bottled up for so
long, but once started Cressida was unable to stop. It
all came pouring out. 'It's Moggy, you see,' she explained. 'If she leaves before she's sixty she can't have
Father's legacy and she depends on that for her old
age...'

'Have you seen the will...?'

'No. Mr Tims, the solicitor, read it out to us but it
was full of heretofores and those long words they use.'

'Just supposing that there had been a misunderstanding about the terms of the legacy, Miss Mogford
would be able to leave, would she not? And you would
be free to leave home, knowing that her future was
secure.'

Cressida gave a great sniff and he glanced at her. She
hardly looked her best, her hair was all over the place,
as far as he could judge she had no make-up on and her
clothes were deplorable. He said very kindly, 'It is likely
that Miss Mogford hasn't understood the conditions of
the legacy. If that could be looked into she might find
herself free to leave before she is sixty. Who exactly told
her of this condition?'

'My stepmother.'

The doctor frowned. Tiresome woman, and how on
earth had he come to get involved in the business? All
the same it seemed to him that he was the only one with
a pair of scissors to cut the tangle. A pity that he would
be leaving the country so soon...

'Feel better?' he asked.

'Yes, thank you.' She put a hand on the door-handle. 'You've been very kind. I won't keep you.'

His hand came down on hers, firm and warm. 'The rest of the day is my own. I'll drive you home.'

At the gates she asked him, 'Would you like to come in? Moggy will make a pot of tea...'

He had got out of the car too and stood looking down at her. 'I should have liked that but I'm going into Yeovil to collect the dog. Have you any ideas about a name?'

'Well, no. Oughtn't he to have a Dutch name since he's to live in Holland?'

'He is English; he should have a name which is common to both countries.'

'Caesar?'

'That would do very nicely. It will suit him, too; he bids fair to be a large beast when he is grown.'

Cressida put out a hand. 'I'm so glad he's going to be looked after. That's wonderful; thank you again for all you've done. Goodbye.'

The hand holding hers felt reassuringly large and secure. She wished very much that the doctor wasn't going away. He would forget her, of course, but knowing him even for such a short time had been pleasant.

He waited by the car until she reached the door and went inside, turning to give a final wave as she did so.

She didn't tell Moggy about the will. First she would write to Mr Tims; it would never do to raise the dear soul's hopes until she had heard from him. Over their tea they talked about the dog and the splendid home he would have when he travelled to Holland.

'Lucky beast,' said Miss Mogford with a good deal of feeling.

*   *   *

Dr van der Linus found his grandmother sitting in her high-backed armchair by a brisk fire. The weather was still fine and sunny, but, as she pointed out cheerfully, arthritis and old age needed warmth.

He bent to kiss her cheek. 'My dear, you are one of those lucky people who never grow old; you're really a very pretty lady, you know.'

'Go on with you! Buttering me up... What have you been doing with yourself?'

'Working.' He sat down opposite her. 'Grandmother, do you know of a Mr Tims of Sherborne?'

'Of course I do. He is my solicitor, has been for years—must be all of seventy.'

'Do you suppose he would allow me the sight of Mr Preece's will?'

'Been to see that girl again, have you?' Lady Merrill's old eyes twinkled with amusement.

'I met her on the road as I was coming here. She looked like a small wet hen. I gave her a lift home and got her to talk. I fancy Mrs Preece has—shall we say?—mis-understood the terms of the will...' He explained briefly and his grandmother nodded in quick understanding.

'So if she has been misleading the girl and the house-keeper things can be put right, the housekeeper can leave and the girl will be free to find herself a job.' Her old face puckered in thought. 'What kind of a job would a wet hen be able to get?'

The doctor laughed. 'I think that if she were free and independent she might begin to look like any other girl. Have you any ideas?'

'I'll think about it. Go and phone George Tims and then come and play cribbage?'

Mr Tims was co-operative. The doctor might pop in any time he chose during the next day. Dr van der Linus went back to the drawing-room and bent his powerful mind to the problem of allowing his grandmother to win without her suspecting it.

Undoubtedly there had been a misunderstanding, Mr Tims assured the doctor the following morning; Miss Mogford was free to leave when she wished and would receive her legacy without delay. 'Mrs Preece will miss her; she has been with the family for many years and will be hard to replace. Mrs Preece is a delicate lady, unable to do a great deal, but of course she will have Cressida—such a sensible girl.'

The doctor agreed blandly and drove back to the house. The little wet hen deserved a chance. She was, he supposed, possessed of the normal skills of a well-educated girl; she should have no difficulty in getting herself a job, but what as? She knew nothing about computers; he felt sure of that. Probably she couldn't type or do shorthand, and she would be no good as a nurse; far too small for a start and with far too soft a heart. Not that he approved of nurses who didn't have soft hearts, that was a vital part of being a decent nurse— but he suspected that she would allow personal sympathy with the patient to supplant nursing expertise. It would have to be something around the house, he thought vaguely. Were there companions nowadays? He wasn't sure, but there were au pairs from whom all that was required was common sense, an ability to do chores around the house, like children and animals and be willing to babysit. He knew that; various of his married friends had them. She would have a roof over her head too...

He was turning in at Lady Merrill's gate when he found the answer.

Over dinner he told his grandmother what he had in mind. 'I shall want your help, my dear,' he added.

Lady Merrill listened carefully. 'This is really rather fun. You do realise that I shall have to do this through a third person? I cannot appear on Mrs Preece's doorstep out of the blue. Let me see, Audrey Sefton knows her. Leave it to me, Aldrik. Is the girl presentable?'

He leaned back in his chair. 'She has a pretty voice and nice manners. Beautiful eyes and no looks. I suppose dressed in the right clothes she would do very well in the most exacting of households.'

'Yes, dear—but how does she get these clothes if she has no money?'

'I'll see Mr Tims. A small sum held in some sort of reserve for her use or something similar.'

His grandmother gave him a sharp look. 'You're going to a great deal of trouble, my dear. She would probably get herself some sort of work if she were left to do so.'

'Oh, I'm sure she would. I shall be going up to Friesland in any case and I'll see Charity and Tyco. Charity might like company for a few months, at least until the baby is born, and that will give Cressida time to look around and decide what she wants to do.'

'Yes, dear? Will you stay up there?'

'I've no appointments there until the middle of the month. I'm tied up in Leiden almost as soon as I get back. That will give me a chance to see something of Nicola...'

'I'm sure she will be pleased to see you again. There's nothing definite, I suppose, dear?'

'No, Grandmother. We are both sensible people; a deep regard and a full knowledge of each other's character seems to me to be essential before marrying.' It sounded pompous but he disarmed her with a grin.

His grandmother gave him a loving look. He was her very favourite grandchild and she wanted him to be happy. He loved his work as a consultant physician and he was very successful. He had money, friends, and those who worked for him liked him. All very well, she thought, but he has no idea what it is like to be in love. Nicola was a cold fish, elegant and witty and wanting, Lady Merrill suspected, only a secure place in her comfortable world, never mind the romance.

He left the next day, promising to come and see her as soon as he could spare a few days. 'I'll be driving Mama over before Christmas,' he promised her.

Two days later Mrs Preece came down to breakfast looking annoyed. 'So vexing—I had planned to go into Yeovil and do some shopping; now that wretched Mr Tims wants to call this morning. Hurry up and eat your breakfast, Cressida, and get a tray ready. If he doesn't stay I'll still have time to go. Bring the coffee as soon as he gets here.'

Cressida went to the kitchen, laid a tray for coffee and told Miss Mogford, 'Half-past ten, he said in his letter. She didn't tell me why, papers to sign, I expect.'

Mr Tims arrived punctually and Mrs Preece, eager to get to Yeovil, didn't keep him waiting. Cressida carried in the coffee, wished him a cheerful good morning and made for the door.

'What I have to say concerns both Cressida and Miss Mogford, Mrs Preece. I should like them both to be here if you would be so kind.'

Mrs Preece flashed him a look quite lacking in kindness. 'Really, Mr Tims, is this necessary? They are both busy around the house.'

Mr Tims looked at her over his spectacles. 'It is necessary, Mrs Preece.'

So Cressida fetched Miss Mogford and they sat awkwardly side by side on one of the big sofas, wondering
what on earth was going to happen next.

Mr Tims cleared his throat and opened his briefcase.
'I was looking through Mr Preece's papers very recently
and it occurs to me that there may have been a misunderstanding concerning Miss Mogford's legacy. Ac-
cording to the will she is entitled to claim it whenever
she wishes; she may in fact leave as soon as she wants
and the money will be paid to her. There is no question
of her having to remain in service until she is sixty. I
believe that was the impression given her at the time of
the reading of the will; mistakenly of course.'

Miss Mogford said gruffly. 'You really mean that? I
can pack my bags and go and still have the legacy?' She
looked at Mrs Preece. 'Madam told me that I would
have to stay or I wouldn't get the money.'

Mrs Preece hastily adjusted her features into a look
of apologetic regret. 'Oh, dear, I'm sure that was never
intended. Silly me, I never have been any good at this
kind of thing.'

She smiled charmingly at Mr Tims, who said politely,
'Well, no harm done, I imagine.' He turned to Cressida.
'If at any future time you should decide to leave home,
I am entrusted with a small sum of money, sufficient, I
trust, to start you off in whatever venture you may
consider.'

'Oh, Cressida would never dream of leaving me,' said
Mrs Preece quickly. 'My nerves, you know. It is essential that I have someone to take care of me and she
is very used to that.'

Cressida said nothing, merely thanked Mr Tims and
offered him more coffee. He refused, and said that he
had another client to see in the neighbourhood, and Miss

Mogford got up to show him out. Mrs Preece bade him goodbye in a cold voice—he hadn't shown her the sympathy she had expected—and Cressida shook hands, saying nothing but looking at him with eyes alight with damped-down excitement. By jove, thought Mr Tims, those lovely eyes of hers made a man forget her ordinary looks.

When he had gone Mrs Preece said sharply, 'Of course there is no question of your going, Miss Mogford. I'm quite prepared to give you a bigger wage, and after all this has been your home for years.'

Moggy's severe features became even more severe. 'You pay me weekly, Mrs Preece. I'm giving you a week's notice as from today.'

She turned on her heel and marched briskly back to the kitchen, leaving Mrs Preece speechless. But not for long!

'The wretch, after all I've done for her. Go after her, Cressida, and tell her she must stay. What am I to do without a housekeeper?' Tears of self-pity rolled down her carefully made-up cheeks.

Cressida, a-fire with the prospect of freedom, sat down on the arm of a chair. 'No, I won't tell Moggy anything of the sort,' she said calmly. 'You've never done anything for her and you can get another housekeeper.'

Mrs Preece's eyes bulged. 'Cressida, have you taken leave of your senses? How dare you talk to me like that, after all I've...?'

She stopped because Cressida was smiling. 'I'm going too, Stepmother.'

'Don't be ridiculous. What will you do? And you've no money.'

'I'm very experienced in housework and Mr Tims said that there was a little money.'

'Rubbish. No one will employ you.' Mrs Preece changed her tactics. 'If you will stay, Cressida, I'll make you an allowance. I'll get another housekeeper and you can train her. I simply cannot manage without someone to run this house. My nerves...' She gave Cressida a wan smile. 'What would your father have said?'

'He would have told me to pack my bags and go,' said Cressida promptly.

Cressida lay awake for a long time that night. She intended to leave at the same time as Moggy although just for the moment she had no idea as to what she would do. London, she supposed vaguely; surely there would be work of some sort there. If she had a roof over her head she could save most of her wages and then train for something, she wasn't sure what. But to be free and live her own life—she uttered a sigh of pure content and fell asleep.

In the light of early morning she lost some of the euphoria. She wasn't sure if she had enough money to get to London, for a start—she would have to see Mr Tims—and when she got there, then where would she go? This was something which would have to be settled before she left home; she was a practical girl; to arrive in London with no notion of where she was to lay her head that night was bird-witted. Something would have to be done about that.

Something was. Mrs Preece, sitting languidly in her drawing-room, refusing to do anything about re-arranging her household, declaring that she felt ill enough to take to her bed, was forced to pull herself together when Miss Mogford came to tell her that she had a caller: Mrs Sefton, who lived some miles from Minton Cracknell but whom she had met on various occasions at other people's houses. She didn't like the lady

overmuch; overbearing, she considered, with an amused
contempt for weak nerves and women who couldn't do
the washing-up for themselves. That she lived in a large
house, well-staffed and well-run, had nothing to say to
the matter; Mrs Sefton was perfectly capable of running
the place single-handed if it were necessary and that
without a single grumble.

She breezed into the room now and bade her reluctant
hostess good morning. Her voice wasn't loud but had a
penetrating ring to it, so that Mrs Preece closed her eyes
for a moment.

'A lovely morning,' declared Mrs Sefton. 'You should
be out. There's the autumn fête at Watly House this
afternoon—aren't you going?'

Mrs Preece said faintly that no, she didn't think she
felt well enough.

'Well, you look all right,' said Mrs. Sefton.

'My nerves, you know.'

Mrs Sefton, who had never quite discovered what
nerves, when mentioned by their possessor, meant, ignored this.

'I'm here to ask a favour. That gel of yours, Cressida,
I've a job for her...'

'She doesn't need a job,' said Mrs Preece, sitting up
smartly.

'I know someone who needs her—an old friend of
mine, Lady Merrill, desperately needs a companion for
a few weeks while her permanent companion has a
holiday.' Mrs Sefton, pleased with her fabrication, added
in ringing tones, 'Not much to do you know—just a few
chores. She's just the one for it. I'm sure you can manage
without her—I don't suppose you see much of her
anyway, she goes out a good deal I dare say.'

'Cressida likes to stay at home with me,' said Mrs. Preece sourly.

'Does she? In that case she'll know just what to do for Lady Merrill. She lives north of Sherborne, quite easy to get at—just the other side of Charlton Horethorne.'

Miss Mogford came in with the coffee and Mrs Preece poured it with a shaking hand. 'I'm quite sure that Cressida won't wish to leave me,' she said in a die-away voice.

'Well, let's have her in to speak for herself,' said Mrs Sefton. She stopped Moggy on her way to the door. 'Ask Miss Preece to come here, will you?'

Mrs Preece opened her mouth to say something tart about guests giving orders in someone else's house and then thought better of it. Mrs Sefton was well known and liked in the county and she was known to give her unvarnished opinion of anyone or anything she didn't approve of. Moggy hurried back to the kitchen where Cressida was making the junket Mrs Preece ate each day—it was supposed to keep the skin youthful, she had been told.

'Drop that, Miss Cressida,' said Moggy urgently, 'you're to go to the drawing-room, there's a Mrs Sefton there, wants to see you.'

'Why?' asked Cressida. 'The junket will curdle...'

'Drat the junket. Your stepmother is in a rage so be careful.'

Cressida might be a plain girl but she was graceful and self-possessed. She greeted Mrs Sefton, grudgingly introduced by Mrs Preece, in a quiet voice, and sat down.

'I've a job for you, my dear,' said Mrs Sefton, not beating about the bush. 'An old lady—a great friend of mine—is in need of a companion for a few weeks and I thought of you. Would you care to take it on?'

'You can't leave me, Cressida,' said Mrs. Preece in a fading voice, 'I shall be ill; besides, it is your place to stay here with me.'

Cressida gave her a thoughtful look and turned sparkling blue eyes upon their visitor. 'I should like to come very much,' she said composedly. 'I have been planning to find a job now that our housekeeper is leaving. When would this lady want me to start?'

Mrs Sefton, primed as to when Miss Mogford was leaving, was ready with an answer. 'Would Thursday be too soon?'

'That is quite impossible,' observed Mrs Preece. 'I have had no replies to my advertisement for a housekeeper and Miss Mogford leaves on the same day. Cressida must stay until I find someone to run the house for me.'

'Oh, surely you can manage to do that yourself?' asked Mrs Sefton. 'I dare say you have outside help from the village?'

Mrs Preece had to admit that she had.

'Well, then, get them to come more often,' said Mrs Sefton cheerfully. 'I dare say you might feel much better if you had something to do.' She smiled in a condescending manner at her hostess. 'And do come to the fête; there's nothing like having an outside interest, you know.'

She got to her feet. 'So be ready on Thursday, Cressida—you don't mind if I call you that? Someone will fetch you directly after lunch.'

She looked at Mrs Preece who wished her a feeble goodbye. 'You must excuse me from getting up,' she whispered dramatically. 'The shock, you know...'

'Well, I don't know,' said Mrs Sefton, 'for I didn't realise that you'd had one. I dare say we shall meet. Do you go out at all socially? I have seen you on several occasions at dinner parties and were you not in Bath last week? At the Royal Crescent, dining with the Croftons? Cressida was not with you?'

'Oh, yes—a long-standing engagement. Cressida hates going out, she is very much a home girl.'

Mrs Sefton raised her eyebrows. 'Then in that case, this little job will give her a taste of the outside world, will it not?'

With which parting shot Mrs Sefton took herself off.

Mrs Preece wept and cajoled and threatened for the rest of that day but to no good purpose. Moggy was adamant about leaving, she packed her things and then went to help Cressida with hers. 'I can't think why you stayed, Miss Cressida, you could have gone months ago...'

'I wasn't going to leave you here, Moggy,' was all Cressida would say.

Miss Mogford stared at her, her arms full of clothes. 'So that's why you've put up with your stepmother's tantrums. I'll not forget that, love. If ever you need help or a home or just someone to talk to, I'll be there waiting and don't you forget it.'

Cressida put down the shoes she was polishing and cast her arms around Miss Mogford. 'Moggy, you are a darling, and I'll remember that and I promise that I'll come to you if I need help or advice or a bed. I shall miss you.'

Moggy's stern countenance softened. 'I shall miss you too after all this time. It hasn't been easy, has it? But everything'll come right now. You really want to go to this old lady?'

'Yes, oh, yes, I do. It's a start, I can get a reference from her and I suppose I'll get paid—I forgot to ask— I'll save all I can and besides Mr Tims said there was a little money for me. I'd better go and see him tomorrow... No, I'll phone, he can send the money here.'

She wrapped her shoes carefully and put them into the shabby suitcase. 'We'd better go and start dinner. Stepmother's alone this evening.'

'Well, don't let her put upon you,' advised Miss Mogford firmly.

Cressida turned eyes shining like stars upon her companion. 'I won't, Moggy, never again.'

CHAPTER THREE

BY LUNCHTIME on Thursday Cressida could feel nothing but relief at leaving her home. Mrs Preece had tried every gambit known to her in her efforts to make Cressida and Miss Mogford change their minds. She had had no success and had resorted to bad temper and reproaches, despite which Cressida had been to the village and arranged for one of the women who came to help in the house to move in temporarily until a new housekeeper could be engaged. She had met the postman on the way and he had given her a letter from Mr Tims—a registered letter containing a hundred pounds and a note—couched in dry-as-dust terms, wishing her well and advising her to use the money prudently until such time as she had a permanent job. Cressida, who hadn't laid hands on anything like that sum for some time, skipped all the way home—rather clumsily because her ankle still pained her at times.

No sooner had she entered the house than her stepmother called to her from the drawing-room. 'Since you're not going until after lunch you might as well get it ready. I'm far too upset to eat much; I'll have an omelette and some thin toast and my usual junket. You had better open a bottle of white wine too.' She picked up the novel she was reading. 'And don't bother to say goodbye, you ungrateful girl. I'll have a tray here.'

Cressida went to the kitchen and found Miss Mogford in the process of getting ready to leave. The baker's van would be calling shortly and the driver was giving her a

47

lift to Templecombe where her sister had a small cottage. Her old-fashioned trunk and cardboard suitcase were already in the hall and as she sat at the kitchen table, wearing her best coat and a rather terrifying hat, she looked as stern as usual but when Cressida joined her her face crumpled.

'That it should come to this—you being turned out of your own home...'

'Well, I've turned myself out, haven't I, Moggy? I hate leaving and so do you but we shall both be a lot happier. After all, it hasn't been much fun since Father died. Has stepmother paid you your wages?'

Miss Mogford nodded. 'I had to ask her for them. And what about you, Miss Cressy? Will you be all right? Supposing this old lady is too much of a handful?'

'Old ladies, on the whole, are rather nice, Moggy, and in any case it's only for a few weeks then I can pick and choose.' Cressida spoke bracingly because Moggy sounded worried, but she felt uncertain of the future, although she had every intention of making a success of whatever she ended up doing. Leaving her home was a sadness she hadn't quite realised, but to stay forever, pandering to her stepmother's whims, was something no longer to be borne. She had been longing for something to happen and now it had and she would make the very best of it.

'There's the baker,' she said, and bustled her old friend out into the hall. 'Now you've got my address and I've got yours, we'll write regularly and as soon as we can we'll have a few hours together.' She put her arms round Moggy's spare frame and hugged her. 'I'm going to miss you dreadfully but you're going to be happy and so am I.' She planted a kiss on the housekeeper's cheek. 'Now off you go. I'll be leaving in an hour or two...'

Miss Mogford spoke gruffly. 'If your poor pa could see you now, he'd turn in his grave. This isn't what he intended.'

'Well, never mind that, Moggy, we're both getting a chance, aren't we? It's rather exciting...'

She walked Miss Mogford out to the van and found that the driver had stowed the luggage in the back, and was waiting to settle his passenger into the front seat. The last Cressida saw of Moggy was her elderly face rigid with suppressed feelings staring out from under that hat.

In the kitchen, warming the milk for the junket, Cressida shed a few tears. She hadn't meant to, they had oozed out from under her lids and she had wiped them away at once. She was going to miss Moggy, she was going to miss her home too and those of her friends whom she saw from time to time, but, she told herself firmly, this was something she had wished for and now it had happened and she must make the most of it. She made the junket, then beat the eggs for the omelette and cut herself a sandwich, for there wouldn't be time for anything more.

Her stepmother was making things as difficult as possible—she wanted fruit and more coffee and a novel she had put down somewhere and simply had to have. Cressida attending to these wants, gobbled her sandwich as she tidied the kitchen just in time to get her elderly tweed coat as a car drew up before the house. Her stepmother's tray hadn't been cleared and nothing had been done about dinner that evening; Cressida, feeling guilty, didn't mind. She went quietly from the old house with her two shabby suitcases and was met on the doorstep by an elderly man with a weatherbeaten face who wished her good day in a friendly voice and stowed her luggage in the boot of the elderly Daimler.

She had gone to the drawing-room on her way out, and, despite Mrs Preece's wish, had been determined to bid her goodbye.

'I told you not to come, Cressida, and as far as I'm concerned you need not bother to return. I wash my hands of you.'

So Cressida got into the car beside the driver and didn't look back, telling herself firmly that she had gone through one of life's doors and shut it behind her.

The driver was friendly and disposed to talk. He was the gardener at Lady Merrill's place, he explained, and besides that he drove the car when it was wanted and did odd jobs around the place. 'Do you drive, miss?' he wanted to know and when Cressida said that yes, she did, although she had seldom had the chance, he gave the opinion that it would be a good thing if she could drive the car sometimes, 'For Lady Merrill doesn't go out often, but when she does I have to leave my garden,' he explained.

'Does her permanent companion drive?' asked Cressida.

He didn't answer at once. 'Er—well, no. You'll be a real blessing.'

'Well, I do hope so. I haven't been a companion before. Will you tell me your name, please?'

'Bert, Miss. There's Mr Baxter, the butler, 'e's old, and Mrs Wiffin the cook and Elsie the parlourmaid, they've all been there, same as me, for nigh on thirty years and no notion of leaving, neither.'

'Lady Merrill is elderly, isn't she? I don't mean to gossip about her, but I don't really know very much about the job.'

'Well, now, Lady Merrill is what you might call elderly, all of eighty-three, but very spry and nothing wrong in the head as you might say. She'll be glad to have someone young around the place.'

'I hope I won't be too young; is her companion elderly?'

'Elderly, oh, yes, miss. Like dogs, do you?'

'Very much.'

'Two Pekinese we've got. Muff and Belle, nice little beasts.'

Cressida was soothed by his amiable talk. By the time they reached Lady Merrill's house she was in good spirits, sustained by the fatherly attitude of Baxter when he opened the door to her.

'Lady Merrill rests in the afternoon,' he told her as he showed her into the hall, 'but Elsie will take you to your room so that you can unpack if you wish. Perhaps a tray of tea? She will let you know when Lady Merrill is awake.'

Elsie was nice too; elderly and thin and wearing an old-fashioned black dress and a white apron. 'You come with me, miss, and I'll bring you a nice pot of tea presently,' she observed, guiding Cressida up the oak staircase at the back of the hall.

The room into which she was shown was charming, not over large but furnished in great comfort. Her case was already there and Elsie said comfortably, 'You just unpack, miss, and I'll be up with your tea in a brace of shakes.'

Left to herself, Cressida peered into cupboards and drawers, put her head round a door to find a small but luxuriously equipped bathroom, and then started to unpack. She hadn't finished when Elsie came back with the tea, nicely arranged on a tray; paper-thin china and a plate of fairy cakes arranged round a small silver teapot. Cressida thanked her and settled down to enjoy the dainty meal; it was a long time since anyone had served her tea on a tray...

An hour later she was led to a room at the front of the house and ushered in by Elsie. 'It's the young lady, my lady,' said Elsie cheerfully. Plainly the staff weren't afraid of their mistress; they weren't familiar either, Cressida had the impression that they were devoted to her.

Lady Merrill was on a day bed, propped up by pillows and cushions and covered with a gossamer fine rug. She looked older than Cressida had expected but there was nothing elderly about her bright eyes and brisk voice.

'Come over here, my dear, where I can see you,' and, when Cressida did so, she examined her from head to foot. 'I hope you will be happy while you are here. Mrs Sefton was so delighted to arrange for you to come here. I believe she knows your stepmother?'

Cressida said cautiously, 'They met at dinner parties and other people's houses. I've met her several times at fêtes and church bazaars.'

'A good-hearted woman! I shall call you Cressida.'

'I should like that, Lady Merrill. Could you tell me what you would like me to do? I—I haven't been a companion before and I'm not sure...'

'Well, now, let me see. I shan't need you until ten o'clock each morning; I breakfast in bed and Elsie helps me dress. I like to read my letters and I expect you to answer them for me, run errands, read to me—my sight isn't very good—and talk. I like to talk. Do you watch television?'

'Well, no, very seldom.' Cressida reflected that there had never been much opportunity for her to do so and the only TV had been in the drawing-room where she had seldom had the time to sit.

'I watch the news,' said Lady Merrill, 'and anything which I consider worthwhile. You shall read the programmes to me each morning so that I can decide if there is anything in which I am interested. You will have your meals with me. Do you play cards or chess?—or cribbage? I enjoy patience...'

'Well, yes, I play chess, not very well and cribbage— I used to play with my father. I'm no good at Bridge.'

'Never mind that—we need four to make a game and I've better things to do than sit around a table bickering over the wrong cards I played.' The old lady nodded. 'You'll do, Cressida.'

Elsie came in with the tea-tray and Lady Merrill said, 'Pour me a cup, my dear, and sit down and have your tea with me.' Nothing loath, Cressida did as she was bid, to be questioned at length as to her life at home and her plans for the future. The questions were put in such a kindly manner that she found herself saying rather more than she intended, although thinking about it afterwards she comforted herself with the thought that since she was unlikely to see Lady Merrill once she had left the house it didn't really matter, and in any case she gave vague and evasive answers which, while not misleading, weren't absolutely true.

She was told to go away and unpack her things and return when the gong sounded for dinner, a meal taken in the old lady's company in a rather dark room, massively furnished. The food was delicious and Lady Merrill, despite her age, an excellent talker. Later, getting ready for bed, Cressida standing at her window, warmly wrapped in her dressing-gown against the chill of the night, watched the moon's fitful beams between the clouds and breathed a great gusty sigh of thankfulness. She surely missed her home and Moggy, but she felt in

her bones at the same time that she would be happy in
this nice old house. For her first job away from home
she hadn't done so badly, she reflected; it was a good
omen for the future. She got into bed and her last waking
thought was that it was a pity she couldn't let Dr van
der Linus know that she had fallen on her feet. He had
been very kind...she wondered sleepily where he was.

Dr van der Linus was sitting in the drawing-room of a
patrician house in Leiden, listening to Nicola van
Germert describing a visit she had paid to friends in
Amsterdam. She had an amusing way of talking although
there was a hint of malice, but he supposed that she
could be forgiven that for it spiced her account just
enough to make those listening to her smile and from
time to time laugh outright. He sat watching her now:
a pretty young woman in her late twenties, self-assured,
well dressed and confident of her place in society. She
would make a good wife, for she had all the attributes
of a good hostess and would have no difficulty in managing his home in Friesland. They had known each other
for some time now and although nothing had been said
their friends were beginning to take it for granted that
they would marry. Indeed, he had taken it for granted
himself; he was thirty-five, time to settle down, although
up until now he had been too immersed in his work to
think of marriage. He supposed that if he had met a girl
and fallen in love...but he hadn't. Perhaps he was getting
too old. He roused himself from his thoughts and joined
in the laughter at one of Nicola's witty remarks, and she
smiled at him with a faintly possessive air.

The party broke up shortly after that and he drove
himself back to the elegant little house he lived in when
he was working in Leiden. He had forgotten Nicola, his

mind already busy with the next day's patients. He let himself in thankfully and went straight to his study, telling his housekeeper to go to bed as he was greeted boisterously by Caesar and a St Bernard dog of immense size. They followed him into the study and settled down by his desk as he picked up his pen. He hadn't written half a dozen words when he put it down again and looked at his watch. It was almost eleven o'clock; his grandmother seldom slept before midnight and there was a telephone by her bed. He dialled her number.

Her voice with its elderly quaver came strongly over the wires. 'Aldrick—I expected you to telephone; you want to know about Cressida?'

'Merely to ask if she has arrived and is settled safely. You don't find her too much of a burden, my dear?'

'On the contrary, she is a charming girl and so anxious to please. She has volunteered no information as to her departure from her home and I think it is unlikely that she will do so—I imagine she has remained silent for so long about her home life that she is unlikely to speak of it to anyone.'

'I shall be going to Friesland in a couple of days, I'll call in on Charity and Tyco and see if they can suggest something. I am most grateful for your help, Grandmother, but the sooner she is settled in a job the better.'

'You think that she will be happy out of England?' Lady Merrill sounded doubtful. 'She seems rather a shy girl.'

'I believe that she will feel safe, at least until she has found her feet. Once she realises that she is free of her stepmother she will probably train for some specific skill, and make a life for herself in England if she wishes.'

'Yes, dear. I'm sure you're right. You've done a good deal for the girl and she is sensible enough to make her own way in the world. She hasn't a boyfriend? Marriage would solve all her problems for her, wouldn't it?'

The doctor frowned. 'I hope that she doesn't meet some unsuitable fellow and imagine herself in love...'

His grandmother, sitting up in bed, turned a chuckle into a cough. 'She is hardly attractive enough for that, Aldrik, though I dare say a visit to the hairdresser and some new clothes will help to improve her appearance.'

'My dear—of course she must be paid. Will you decide on a suitable wage and let me know?'

'Yes, of course. Weekly, I think. I suspect that she has very little money.'

'Yes, well, I'll leave that to you.'

'Yes, dear.' She bade him goodnight and he put the receiver down. 'That's settled,' he told the dogs. 'Now I can forget about her.' Charity was bound to know of someone who would employ the girl...

He had a teaching round in the morning, private patients to see in the early afternoon and an outpatients clinic afterwards. He was pleasantly tired when he got home again; an hour at his desk and then he would drive himself and the dogs out of Leiden and walk for an hour. He opened his front door, called to his housekeeper that he was home and waited while she came to meet him. Mies was elderly, rather bony, and despite this she contrived to look cosy. She said now, 'You've had a long day—you'll be tired. There's Juffrouw van Germert waiting for you in the drawing-room—I'll bring a pot of coffee.'

He gave her a smiling reply, fending off the two dogs. He had been looking forward to a quiet evening but good manners forbade him from saying so. He went into his drawing-room with the dogs and Nicola called across the room from the chair where she was sitting. 'I thought you might like company after your busy day. All those people and so uninteresting and dull I dare say.'

She didn't get up but held up a hand. 'How about taking me to the Hague for a meal? I've had such a boring day...'

He sat down in his winged chair opposite to her. 'Tell me about it,' he invited.

'Well, that's just it, there's nothing to tell—I did some shopping and had coffee with friends and this afternoon I went to the hairdressers.'

'Perhaps if you had some kind of a job you would find the days pass more quickly?'

She opened her eyes wide. 'Work? Aldrik, I couldn't possibly. To sit in an office all day would be so boring and I'm far too sensitive to be any good at social work of any kind. Besides I don't need——' She was interrupted by the telephone ringing, and the doctor picked up the receiver.

It was Lady Merrill, telling him that she had had a splendid day, that Cressida had been a delightful companion and that they were making plans to drive around the countryside each day while the weather was fine. 'Such an industrious girl, too,' said his grandmother. 'Baxter is enchanted by her and Elsie is so relieved to have someone young to run up and downstairs when I forget something...'

The doctor laughed. 'She sounds a treasure. You think I've done the right thing! I'll see Charity and Tyco very shortly and you can sound her out about coming over here?' He put the phone down presently and turned to find Nicola looking at him intently. She smiled at once, though, and said at her most charming, 'Who is this

mysterious girl and why must you talk to the van der
Bronses? They live near your place in Friesland, don't
they? Is she an au pair?'

Dr van der Linus sat down in his chair again. Nicola
looked interested and for some reason he wanted to talk
about Cressida. He told her how he had met her and the
chain of events which had led him to engineer her escape
from what had become an untenable life. 'She is a
charming girl, no looks to speak of but beautiful eyes
and a gentle voice. My grandmother is delighted with
her but of course she can't stay there for long; she sup-
poses that she is filling a gap while my grandmother's
companion is on holiday. My idea was to find her a job
away from that stepmother of hers where she can feel
safe, save some money and decide what she wants to do.
The van der Bronses know any number of people; I'm
sure they could help.'

Nicola had listened without interrupting at all, her face
half turned away so that he didn't see the thoughtful
suspicion on it. She had been sure of him and a delightful carefree future; it only needed a small push on
her part at the right moment—but now there was a tiny
cloud on her horizon: this girl, this plain girl with the
eyes was obviously taking more than a fair share of his
thoughts and if she went to Friesland he would probably
see her frequently. She thought fast.

'Aldrik,' she turned an eager sympathetic face to him,
'never mind the van der Bronses, I know the very thing
for this nice girl. Tante Clotilde, remember her?
Jonkvrouw van Germert—she lives in Noordwijk-aan-
Zee. Near enough for you to keep on eye on her; besides
there are any number of English living there and she'll
quickly make friends. Tante Clotilde was only saying last
week that she wanted a companion, and having an

English girl would make it so much more interesting for her.'

She saw the doubt on his face. 'Can you spare the time to go with me and see her soon? There's no need to say anything about this girl until you're satisfied that she might like the job. What is her name?'

'Cressida, Cressida Preece.'

'A pretty name—Shakespeare, isn't it? I wonder why?'

'I've no idea. It might be a good idea. I'm going up to Friesland in a day or two but when I come back—in a week's time—we might visit your aunt. I should feel happier if I knew Cressida was settled somewhere where I can see her from time to time. I feel responsible for her although I am not sure why.'

Nicola allowed herself a sweet smile as she began making plans. She was a clever young woman; she didn't see Aldrik again before he went to his home, but once he had gone she got into her sports car and roared the short distance to Noordwijk-aan-Zee and spent an hour with her aunt...

The doctor drove himself and the dogs north. It was a cold evening and already getting dark and there was little to see of the country through which he travelled, only the dim outline of farms with their great barns attached to them and the gleam of the water from time to time. He had gone over the Afsluitdijk and taken the road towards Leeuwarden, turned north again before he reached the town and joined the road to Dokkum, to turn off again, this time on to a narrow brick road which led him at length to a small village, seven or eight miles from the Waddenzee: a cluster of small houses, a large, austere church and a small school building, all shrouded in darkness, and half a mile beyond the wrought-iron gates which were the entrance to his home.

Wester was waiting for him, a stoutly built, very tall man with a rugged face and blond hair with a heavy sprinkling of grey. He had the door of the house open before the doctor reached it and the two men shook hands. Wester was the best part of ten years older than the doctor and they had known each other since boyhood; Wester's father had been house steward to the doctor's father and when his own father had died he had stepped into his shoes, and since he had married the doctor's cook some five years previously and had two sons it stood to reason that when their time came one or other of them would take over from his father, an arrangement which was satisfactory to everyone concerned.

They stood in the open doorway for a few minutes while the dogs roamed free and the doctor slipped naturally into the language of his youth and spoke Fries, looking around him at the large hall beyond the vestibule where the portraits of his ancestors hung on its white walls, and the wide staircase swept up to the gallery above his head. It was good to be home, he reflected, and the unbidden thought that Cressida would like it crossed his mind. She would like the house in Leiden too, he conceded, small compared with this but charming and old and splendidly furnished. He frowned, whistled to the dogs and went inside while Wester fetched his case from the car and then drove it round to the garage at the back of the house.

He was halfway across the hall when Tyske, Wester's wife, came through the door at the back of the hall to meet him. She was a tall strongly built woman with mild blue eyes and a wide smile, and she broke into speech when she saw him; it was a delight to have him home again and there was a splendid supper waiting for him, he had only to say...

He flung a great arm round her shoulders and lapsed into Fries once more, asking her about the children and whether the cat and the pet rabbits were well, and presently he crossed the hall to his drawing-room, a vast room with a lofty ceiling and tall wide windows draped in russet velvet. There was a stone fireplace, hooded, at one end of the room and some magnificent bow-fronted display cabinets filled with pretty porcelain and silver. The chairs and sofas were large and comfortable, there were lamp tables and a vast rent table between the windows and amber shaded lamps. A log fire burned brightly and the lamp-light cast shadows on the silk-panelled walls hung with more portraits and landscapes. The doctor stood a moment, enjoying the room, and then went to sit by the fire; this was his home, he had been born there and lived in it as a boy and although he traveled a good deal nowadays he came back to it with content.

It was a large house and very old, with its steepled roof and odd little towers, rows of small windows under the tiles and chimneys, too large for a man to live in alone, but his father had died within the last few years and his mother was on a long visit to one of his sisters in France, and when she returned, she had told him, if he were to marry, she would prefer to live in the house at Dokkum which she had inherited from her father. 'I hope you will marry soon, my dear,' she had told him. He had smiled and said that at the moment he had no wish to marry; his work took him to major hospitals in his own country as well as in Europe and beyond, true, he was a lecturer at Leiden Medical School and had a number of beds at the hospital, he lectured in Groningen

too and he had beds at Leeuwarden, but he went frequently to England for consultations, and, indeed, had
travelled on various occasions to America, the Far East
and Russia; none the less most of his work was in
Holland, a small enough country for him to live, if he
wished, here, in his house, and travel with ease to Leiden,
Amsterdam and den Haag.

He was summoned presently by Wester and crossed
the hall to have his supper in the small room he used as
a dining-room unless he had guests. It was cosy, with
an old-fashioned stove, a round table and a small side-
board, lighted by wall sconces. He ate an excellent meal,
a dog on either side of him, and then went to his study,
a room at the back of the house overlooking the gardens,
bare now at the approach of winter, merging into the
polder land beyond. Here he settled down to work, pre-
paring for a series of lectures that he was to give in
Groningen and checking his appointments in
Leeuwarden. It was late when he went upstairs to bed
and the house was very quiet, the dogs, coming in from
a last run in the grounds, settled down in their baskets
in the warm kitchen. Wester and Tyske had long since
gone to bed and the wind sighed in the trees and when
he opened his window the air was crisp and very cold.
Winter could be hard in Friesland but the doctor liked
it that way. He slept the sleep of a tired man without
thinking once of Nicola. He did, however, dream of
Cressida.

Cressida didn't dream of him, but she did think of him
quite a lot. She had settled down very nicely to her duties,
none of them heavy—most of them weren't duties,
anyway; she didn't consider that taking the dogs for a
walk was a duty, and since she shared Lady Merrill's

taste in literature reading out loud was a pleasure. Here were all the books she had never had the time to read during the last two years and in variety. Lady Merrill's taste was catholic; Cressida read Trollope, P.D. James, Alastair Maclean and then large chunks of John Donne, Herrick and Keats and then back to romance—Mary Stewart, and odd chapters of *Jane Eyre* interlarded with books on antiques, about which Lady Merrill knew a great deal, and when these palled Cressida was bidden to fetch the heavy leather-covered albums filled with photos of Lady Merrill's youth.

They talked too, long conversations about clothes, the theatre and how to put the world to rights, but none of their talks revealed anything of Lady Merrill's own family and Cressida was too polite to ask.

She hadn't been so happy for a long time; her days were nicely filled, she was being useful but she wasn't being browbeaten, meals were delicious and Baxter and the rest of the staff were kind. She lost her thinness after the first week and her cheeks were delicately pink. In her purse she had a week's wages as well as the hundred pounds and in response to Lady Merrill's delicate hints she took herself off to Yeovil and bought a tweed skirt, a couple of blouses and a pretty woollen jumper and, since she had become sensitive about the only decent dress she owned and which she donned each evening to compliment Lady Merrill's dark silks and velvets, she went to Laura Ashley and bought a dark red velvet dress, long-sleeved and simple but suitable for the dinner table. She spent rather more than she had meant to but she consoled herself with the thought that when she left Lady Merrill's she would have the nucleus of a suitable wardrobe for the kind of job she could do. She suspected that not all companion's jobs would be as pleasant as this one, but she would have a roof over her head and money in her pocket.

Studying her much improved reflection in her bedroom looking-glass, Cressida allowed herself to think about Dr van der Linus. It was a pity that he couldn't see her now in the red dress. The suspicion that he had pitied her rankled rather; she would have liked to show him that she wasn't normally a wispy creature with a sprained ankle...

Which wasn't how Lady Merrill described her a few nights later, sitting up in bed, chatting with the doctor on the phone. 'Of course I'm not asleep, dear,' she protested, 'you know that I never sleep so early in the night. You want to know about Cressida?' She rearranged her bedjacket and smiled to herself. 'Yes, I quite understand that you still feel responsible for her. She is well and, I believe, happy. She is a delightful companion and such a help to us all. She seemed to me to be a plain girl but she has improved in looks during these last few days. A good thing; she has a far better chance of finding employment now that she has a little colour in her cheeks and is putting on weight. It is surprising what good food does for one.'

'I'm grateful to you, Grandmother, and I hope you will shortly be able to go back to your usual way of life. I mentioned her to Nicola and she tells me that she knows just the person to employ Cressida. An aunt of hers, lives at Noordwijk-aan-Zee and needs a companion. She sounds just what is needed and so much more satisfactory if she is someone who is known to Nicola. You don't think that I am interfering with Cressida's future? I should like to think that she had a good job...'

'Well, Aldrik, the alternative is to cast the girl loose into the world to find her own way. She might be lucky;

on the other hand she might not. At least we shall know where she is.' Lady Merrill frowned thoughtfully. 'This aunt, have you met her?'

'Not yet, but I shall go and see her with Nicola when I get back to Leiden. I've a clinic there next week.'

'You will write and let her know?'

'No. I fancy that if she knew what we have contrived she might well refuse. How about getting hold of Mrs Sefton again?'

'A good idea—mutual friends in Holland and so on. That should do very well. Let me know your plans in good time. You're happy at Janslum?'

'Yes, Grandmother. I've been at Groningen all day; tomorrow I shall be in Leeuwarden and plan to go back to Leiden at the end of the week.'

'When will you be over here again?'

'There's a seminar in a month's time—I shall see you then.'

She said goodnight and lay back on her pillows, her elderly mind busy. Somehow she didn't like the sound of Nicola's aunt, but there was nothing much she could do about that; perhaps she was misjudging Nicola, a young woman she didn't like and who, as far as she knew, had never put herself out to do anyone a kindness unless it was of benefit to herself.

Lady Merrill lay and thought about that until at last she went to sleep.

CHAPTER FOUR

OCTOBER had slipped into November, bringing colder weather and dark evenings. Lady Merrill was content to sit indoors or walk, well wrapped up, in the grounds of the house. It was Cressida who took the dogs for their walk each morning and evening, bundled in her old mac and wearing a scarf over her mousy locks. She enjoyed these walks, her head full of plans, mostly about clothes and, rather worriedly, about her future. Lady Merrill hadn't told her how long she was to stay and when she mentioned the companion to anyone they were vague as to when she would return. Surely she would be given a week's notice at least? she thought. All the same, given the day off, she took herself to Yeovil, purchased a copy of the *Lady* magazine and studied the adverts. There was no lack of urgent requests for mother's helps and nannies and a fair sprinkling of appeals for kind persons to cope with old ladies, old gentlemen or the housework. It shouldn't be too difficult to find another job. She marked the most promising of these over a cup of coffee and a bun and took herself off to the shops. She had another week's wages in her purse, to be laid out with care; shoes—she couldn't afford boots—and undies. She still had the hundred pounds intact so that next week's wages could be spent on another sweater, gloves and a handbag. Thus equipped, she felt, she would pass muster for a start, gradually gathering together a suitable wardrobe. When her father had been alive, she had bought nice clothes, for he had been generous to her,

66

but now they had seen their best days although her coat was well cut and of good quality and was good for another winter or so.

She went back to Lady Merrill, well pleased with her modest prudent purchases, ate dinner in the old lady's company and spent an hour allowing her to win a game of cribbage before Elsie came to help her to bed.

'I shall miss you,' declared the old lady as Cressida wished her goodnight.

'I shall miss you too, Lady Merrill, but you'll have your companion back again and I'm sure you will be glad to see her once more.'

Lady Merrill looked vague. 'Yes, yes, I suppose I shall.' She trotted off on the faithful Elsie's arm and Cressida, with nothing better to do, went to her room and tried on the new shoes.

Once in her bed, nicely propped up with pillows and the necessities for the night on the bedside table, Lady Merrill picked up the telephone. It was barely ten o'clock and high time that she had a chat with Audrey Sefton. A night-bird herself, the old lady had no compunction about rousing such of her friends with whom she wished to gossip; fortunately Mrs Sefton hadn't gone to bed and listened with growing interest to what Lady Merrill had to say.

'But my dear, I don't know this woman...'

'Well, of course you don't,' said Lady Merrill testily, 'But if Aldrik says she's all right then that's all that matters. The thing is to let Cressida think that it is a job that someone you know, however vaguely, happened to have heard about—mutual friends and so on. Go on, Audrey, Aldrik is anxious to get the girl settled.'

'Yes, but why in Holland?'

'He won't lose touch...' Lady Merrill chuckled and heard her friend draw a breath.

'You don't mean...?'

'I don't mean anything. Will you do it?'

'Very well, although I dislike subterfuge as you very well know.'

'There is a very good reason. I'll let you know what Aldrik says. Goodnight, Audrey, and thank you.'

The old lady settled back into her pillows, well pleased with herself.

It was the best part of a week before the doctor returned to Leiden and had the leisure to visit Nicola's aunt. It was a cold grey afternoon when he picked her up from her parents' house in den Haag and drove up the coast to Noordwijk-aan-Zee, and the house, when they reached it, looked as bleak as the day, wilting rapidly into an even colder evening. It was a fair-sized villa, built some fifty years previously; red brick and a great deal of fancy stonework, and surrounded by a garden, meticulously neat, bordered by shrubs and empty flowerbeds. The doctor found it dispiriting.

Jonkvrouw van Germert received them graciously, offered weak milkless tea and minuscule biscuits and assured them that she was delighted to see them. 'I lead a secluded life,' she observed, 'and at times I am lonely.'

Nicola sipped her tea, with every appearance of enjoyment. 'Tante Clotilde,' she began hesitantly, 'you say you're lonely. I suppose you wouldn't consider having a companion?'

Her aunt looked surprised. She did it very well, having rehearsed the whole conversation with Nicola. 'A companion?' She tittered. 'Am I quite old enough for that,

Nicola? I don't need anyone to pick up my dropped stitches or read aloud; my eyes are still good.'

Nicola laughed gently. 'I didn't mean that kind of companion, Tante, but someone to accompany you on walks and drive the car, an intelligent woman who can listen as well as talk—in fact, someone to be in this house with you.' She added lightly, 'You told me yourself that you were considering it.'

Jonkvrouw van Germert appeared to think. 'I must say that put like that it sounds attractive, especially during the winter months. But why do you ask, Nicola?'

The doctor hadn't spoken. Now he said, 'I know of an English girl who is anxious to find a pleasant situation. She is at present with my grandmother, who is very pleased with her. She doesn't speak Dutch, of course, but that might be of added interest to you. She is, for lack of a better word, that old-fashioned thing, a lady, intelligent, and, from what my grandmother tells me—and she usually knows—a very kind and considerate girl.'

'Surely she would prefer to stay in her own country?'

'She has few friends and no immediate family. Aldrik thinks that it might benefit her to have a change of scene. However, I won't bother you further, Tante; Aldrik has any number of friends, he can ask around...'

Her aunt appeared to consider. 'I must say that the idea appeals to me. Not permanently, of course, but for the winter months, and by then this girl may find employment which is more suitable or start to train for something. I'd like to think about it.' She gave the doctor a gracious smile. 'I'll let you know within the next day or so.'

'I'm sure Tante Clotilde will decide to employ this girl,' said Nicola as they drove back to den Haag, 'and if she doesn't you can still ask the van der Bronses to look around. I hear Charity is expecting a child.'

'In a couple of months. They're delighted.' They began to talk of other things until he dropped her off at her home, refusing to go in with her with the plea of work to be done and a late visit to an ill patient in the hospital.

Nicola pecked his cheek—she disliked what she called 'demonstrative behaviour'—and he got into his car again and drove back to Leiden, dismissing her from his thoughts. He felt uneasy; Jonkvrouw van Germert was the answer to his scheme, and yet he wasn't satisfied. He didn't like her, although there had been no reason for his dislike. Her home was hideous, he considered, over-furnished and yet uncomfortable; on the other hand the surroundings were pleasant and he would be near enough to make sure that Cressida was happy. If she wasn't it would be easy enough to find something else. Of course she might refuse to leave England, but he thought it unlikely; she had had no experience at finding work and she had little money. There was no need for him to worry; he parked the car at the hospital and went to see his patient.

Although he told himself time and again that his interest in Cressida was purely derived from a wish to see someone unfortunate made happy, he might have felt the need to worry if he had overheard the conversation Nicola had with her aunt over the phone.

It was a couple of days later when Lady Merrill said suddenly in the middle of lunch. 'My—er—my companion will be returning in a week, Cressida, and I have been giving the matter some thought. Have you any plans?'

Cressida put her fork carefully down on the plate. 'No—no, I haven't, Lady Merrill, but I have no doubt that I shall be able to find something.'

Cressida cast around in her head. There was an aunt of her mother's living somewhere in Cumbria whom she had never seen, two cousins in Canada and another cousin in the States, all much older than she. 'Well, I'm sure I can find a room,' she began, 'just for a little while, you know.'

'Mrs Sefton—you know her, of course—telephoned me yesterday and asked after you, and, when I mentioned that you would be leaving shortly, wanted to know if you were interested in a job in Holland as companion to a lady living on her own. Middle-aged, I believe and speaks fluent English. She lives very comfortably by the sea. Not a permanent position but for the winter months.'

'Does Mrs Sefton know this lady?'

'No, but she knows an acquaintance of hers who mentioned it in a letter.' Lady Merrill smiled encouragingly. 'It might be better to go to someone already known rather than to a complete stranger.'

That made sense, reflected Cressida; besides, it would be nice to go abroad—and Dr van der Linus lived there. She had her passport too.

Lady Merrill watched the tell-tale expressions drift across Cressida's face; she wasn't going to say any more, she had already been involved in Aldrik's plans and told far too many fibs as well as inventing a mythical companion, but she hoped that Cressida would go to Holland because that was what he wanted, although she was sure that he didn't know why he wanted it. She could be wrong about that. She wasn't quite happy about this woman being an aunt of Nicola's; on the other hand Aldrik would be able to see Cressida from time to time and for the present she was content with that; besides, he had seen this woman and approved of her.

Cressida had made up her mind. 'I think I'd like to take this job. It will be a change to see another country. Does this lady wish me to write to her?'

'That would be a good idea. I'll get the address from Mrs Sefton.'

So Cressida wrote a brief polite letter and received one by return of post, couched in pleasant terms and offering a wage which was ample for her needs. She was expected in a week's time and directions as to how she was to get there were added. Very satisfactory, thought Cressida, suppressing a feeling of uneasiness which she couldn't account for. It had all been so easy, but she brushed the doubt aside; she was in no position to look a gift horse in the mouth.

She went to Yeovil once more on a free afternoon and added to her wardrobe a plain jersey dress in grey which she hoped would pass muster for more formal occasions, a pair of court shoes, going cheap in a closing-down sale, and another sweater. She had, she considered, an adequate wardrobe which she proceeded to pack in her two cases which Elsie had taken away and dusted and polished for her. The last day came and she got out of bed feeling sad and rather reluctant to go. She had been happy with Lady Merrill and the entire household had been kind and friendly. She hoped that Jonkvrouw van Germert would be as kind.

'I shall miss you, child,' observed Lady Merrill. 'I hope you will be happy in Holland—write to me, won't you?' She offered an elderly cheek for Cressida's kiss. Baxter and Elsie bade her a reluctant goodbye too as they saw her into the car which was to take her to Yeovil and the train to London. Her travelling expenses had been sent, although there had been no allowance made for taxis or meals on the way. She was to travel to Harwich and take the night ferry to the Hoek. It seemed to her a needlessly round-about journey, especially as she had to cross London, but she had her instructions and presumably was expected to keep to them. At the Hoek she was to catch a train to den Haag and change again to a local train to Noordwijk-aan-Zee where she was to take a taxi to Jonkvrouw van Germert's house. In the train speeding up to Waterloo, she read the instructions once again and then settled down to watch the scenery, wondering when she would see it again. Probably in the spring, she reminded herself, for it had been made clear that she was to be employed only for the winter months. She wondered briefly about her stepmother, who hadn't replied to her letters, but she had had long letters from Moggy, happily settled with her sister and reiterating her offer to Cressida of a place to stay if ever she should need one. It was a comforting thought.

Cressida had travelled in Europe with her father before he remarried; France, Italy and Greece, and always in comfort, so that she was unprepared for the inside cabin she was to share with three other women on the ferry, and since she had to be careful of her money she made do with coffee and a ham roll before she climbed into her bunk. The three other occupants were older women, one of whom snored. She had a wakeful night and got up as early as she dared, washed and dressed by the aid of one small light and went on deck. It had been a rough crossing and the wind was blowing but after the stuffiness of the cabin she was glad of the fresh air. They were very near the Hoek now; she went and got herself a cup of tea and a roll and collected her luggage.

There weren't a great many passengers, she was quickly through Customs and the train was waiting in the station. It was a short journey to den Haag but she wasted a good deal of time looking for the right platform, unable to hurry with her two cases, and it was with relief that she settled in the train for Noordwijk-aan-Zee. Much revived by a cup of coffee, she watched the scenery until the ticket collector came round, pointing out in good English that the train didn't go to the little town but to the larger Noordwijk inland. 'You can get a taxi from the station,' he told her cheerfully. 'It is two kilometres, no distance.'

Which she was glad to discover was true; what was more, the taxi driver understood English and knew where Jonkvrouw van Germert lived. He drove through the wide aged gate up to the front door, got out and put her cases on the step, accepted his fare and a tip, wished her a happy stay and drove away as she rang the bell.

The door was opened by a cross-looking woman who stared at her without speaking but when Cressida uttered her mistress's name she stood back while Cressida, lugging her suitcases, went into the hall, then she walked away to disappear through a door on one side of the hall.

A gloomy place, thought Cressida, but obviously a well-to-do household if the heavy side-table and side-chairs, the thick carpet and the elaborate chandelier were anything to go by.

The girl came back, said, '*Kom mee,*' and led the way back across the hall and opened a door for Cressida to go through. The room she entered was as gloomy as the hall, rich brown and terracotta with a great deal of dark furniture. There was a fire opposite the door and a woman sitting in the chair drawn up to it.

'Come in, then—Miss Preece, isn't it? How do you do?'

Cressida crossed to the chair and offered a hand. 'Jonkvrouw van Germert?'

'Yes.'

Her hand was shaken after a moment's hesitation. 'Well, Corrie had better show you your room—lunch is at half-past twelve and we can talk then.'

She frowned slightly. 'You are very slight—I hope you are strong?'

'Oh, yes.' Cressida eyed her companion, a stout florid lady, very fashionably dressed, and wondered why she needed to be strong.

'Well, find Corrie and get unpacked; you have almost an hour.'

So Cressida went back into the hall and found Corrie standing at the front of the stairs. They each took a case and climbed to the square landing, where Corrie opened a door at the end of a narrow passage. The room looked over the garden at the back of the house and that was the best part about it. It was a small room, adequately furnished and cold, and there was a bathroom next to it. Left to herself, Cressida poked her nose into cupboards and drawers, tried the bed and looked out of the window. Of course, she told herself, it was a grey day; when the sun shone the room would look much nicer and once she had settled in she would have a vase of flowers and perhaps a small table lamp by the bed. She had some photos of her mother and father and her home—the place would soon be more cheerful, it was only that after the comfort of her room at Lady Merrill's house this one seemed a little bare.

She unpacked quickly, did her face and hair, and, mindful of the time, went back downstairs.

Over lunch Jonkvrouw van Germert outlined Cressida's duties, which were rather different from those at Lady Merrill's. She was to keep her own room clean and of course make her bed, water the many plants and arrange the flowers, wash the porcelain in the display cabinets in the drawing-room, answer the phone if the maid was out or busy, make sure that the daily cleaning woman had done her work properly and make herself useful as and when necessary.

'And my free day?' asked Cressida.

'A free day? Oh, do you expect that? But you will be living here in comfort with me, and I have no free day.'

Jonkvrouw van Germert saw the look on Cressida's face and made haste to change her tactics. It would never do for the girl to leave after dear Nicola had planned everything so carefully. 'Well, let me see, I go to the Bridge club on Wednesdays; supposing you consider yourself free to go out from 10 o'clock in the morning until seven o'clock in the evening?'

It seemed there was to be no question of an hour or two off each day and perhaps it would be sensible to wait for a few days before suggesting it. Cressida agreed, and then asked in her sensible way, 'And my salary? Is that to be paid weekly or monthly?'

'Oh, monthly. Now that we have decided on these tiresome details will you be good enough to come upstairs with me? I rest for an hour after lunch and you may read to me. My English is good,' said Jonkvrouw van Germert with a lamentable lack of modesty, 'but you will read slowly; if I do not understand a passage you will explain it to me.'

It had been a long day, thought Cressida, getting ready for bed that night and jumping into her bed, thankful for the hot-water bottle which Corrie had surprisingly found and filled for her. She wasn't as cross as she looked—probably she was tired, for there was certainly enough for her to do. The house wasn't over large but it was full of furniture and knick-knacks and the floors were polished wood. There was a cook; Cressida had been sent to the kitchen to fetch a fresh pot of coffee and had seen her there. She had offered a hand and the surprised woman had shaken it, giving her an unfriendly glance and muttering something in Dutch. Not a cheerful household, reflected Cressida, curling her small person around the warmth of the bottle; probably they had thought her coming would make more work for them but judging from the list of tasks she was expected to get through each day she might turn out to be a help.

She was disappointed, but that, she told herself firmly, was because Lady Merrill had been exceptionally kind. She would doubtless have her ups and downs but she had a roof over her head, quite a good salary and a chance to save some of it. Just before she dropped off she thought that she might, by some miracle, meet Dr van der Linus again, then she slept.

Her days, she discovered, were fully occupied—making herself useful covered a multitude of odd jobs as well as being Jonkvrouw van Germert's companion and at her beck and call—but she had the odd half-hour to herself from time to time when visitors called. She had arrived on a Thursday so that she had to wait a week for her free day and when it came at last it brought cold rain and a bitter wind. Not that Cressida minded that; she tidied her room, ate her breakfast, went to Jonkvrouw van Germert's room to bid her good morning and was told in a chilly voice to be sure and be back by seven o'clock, and then she ran down to the kitchen. Her Dutch was fragmental but she managed, *'Bood-*

schappen?' which she had learned meant shopping, and
pointed at Corrie and the cook in turn.

They stared at her for a moment and then smiled and
nodded, and she waited while they wrote what they
wanted on a bit of paper.

'*Geld*?' asked Corrie.

She smiled again at once when Cressida said, '*Straks*,'
which was a useful word she had made haste to learn
since it meant later, presently or even not now.

The bus service was good though not so frequent in
the winter months; all the same it took her swiftly to
Leiden, where, Jonkvrouw van Germert had told her in
one of the more expansive moments, there was a good
deal to see and even some nice shops. She had added,
'And if you want the cheaper places, there is Hema,
rather like your Woolworths, I believe...' A remark
which had annoyed Cressida very much.

In Leiden she went straight to the tourist office to get
a map of the town and all the information she could
find, and, thus armed, set out to enjoy herself. She had
had to admit to herself within the first few days of living
at the villa that she wasn't very happy there; Jonkvrouw
van Germert didn't like her. Not that she had ever said
so but her indifference was plain to see and she treated
Cressida with a kind of long-suffering politeness which
was hard to bear. Almost as though she didn't want a
companion and certainly not me, Cressida had thought.
What she really needed was another maid in the house;
Corrie was overworked and the woman who came in to
clean had no time to do more than polish the floors and
clean the kitchen, and she herself discovered that she
was expected to make beds, dust and occasionally set
the table for meals. It was a job, she told herself stoutly,
and it enabled her to see something of another country,

and having a day off to herself once a week was something to look forward to.

She followed one of the leaflet's instructions and spent an hour or more at the Lakenhal before going in search of coffee. From the café she found her way to Breestraat running through the heart of the oldest part of the city, bent on viewing the old fortification, the Burcht, and that done she made her way to the Korenbeursbrug to enjoy the views her leaflet urged her to see. She looked her fill, and then, bent on seeing the Sint Pieterskerk, walked back towards Breestraat. It was as she was waiting to cross the street that she saw Dr van der Linus on the opposite pavement. She stood quite still, jostled by impatient people wishing to cross the street and finding her in the way. She was unaware of them, wholly taken up with the delight of seeing him again. He had crossed the street before she had decided what to do. His, 'Cressida, what a delightful surprise,' was uttered with just the right air of unexpectedness; he had been in France for two weeks and had returned several days before he was expected, and although he had planned to call on Nicola's aunt in order to make sure that Cressida had settled down nicely he had not expected to see her in Leiden. He took her hand and smiled kindly at her. 'You look well...'

'I've a job here, companion to a lady who lives in Noordwijk-aan-Zee.'

'You're happy? You don't find it strange?' He gave her a sharp glance. 'This lady is kind to you?'

It would have been a relief to tell him that she wasn't happy and that everything was strange and the lady was rather less than kind, but that would never do. She said in her quiet way, 'It is a little strange but everyone, or almost everyone, speaks English. I've only been here for a week. Noordwijk-aan-Zee is very attractive; I dare say it's very busy in the summer.'

He frowned a little, watching her face, sure that she would have liked to have said more but wasn't going to. It was a pity that he was on his way to the hospital and already late. 'It would have been nice to have had lunch together,' he told her, 'but I am late already. Let me have your address...'

She gave it to him and added, 'But please don't come and see me, I'm not sure if Jonkvrouw van Germert would like that.'

'Oh, why is that?'

'You're going to be very late for your appointment,' said Cressida. 'I dare say we shall meet again when there's more time.'

He took her hand in his. 'Indeed we will, I don't intend to lose sight of you.'

She watched him stride away, going towards the Rapenburg Canal and the medical school and she went on her way to the church. It was vast and empty and she perched on a solitary chair the better to think. It had been wonderful seeing the doctor again and surprising too. She had thought that he lived in Friesland but apparently he came to Leiden, she presumed to the hospital, and it wasn't very likely that she would see him again for some time. Even if she came to Leiden each week on her day off the chances of meeting him there were remote, but all the same she was aware of a warm, comforting glow at the thought that he had remembered her and stopped to talk even though it had been obvious to her that he was in a tearing hurry.

The church was cold; she walked back to Breestraat and had a cheese roll and coffee in a little café and went to look at the shops. She wasn't to be paid until the end

of the month so her purchases were small and necessary
but with Christmas approaching the shops had plenty
in their windows. She spent a happy hour wandering
from one to the other, deciding what she would buy at
the end of the month, then had tea and a mouth-watering
mountain of a cream cake before catching the bus back.
She had enjoyed her day and as she stood on the step
waiting for Corrie to open the door she reflected that
perhaps she had been over-hasty in her first impression
of Jonkvrouw van Germert; after all, they had to get to
know each other. She went straight to the kitchen and
handed over the purchases she had made for Corrie and
the cook and then hurried to her room to tidy herself
for the evening. Her employer changed each evening;
Cressida got into the grey dress which would have to be
worn until she had her wages and she could buy a second
one. Perhaps if she went to the Hague on one of her
free days she would find something to suit her pocket.

Jonkvrouw van Germert was in the drawing-room,
wearing an elaborate dress and a good deal of gold
jewellery. 'Oh, you're back,' she observed as Cressida
went in. 'I shall be out for dinner—the car will be here
at any minute now. I have told Cook that you can have
your supper in the kitchen with her and Corrie—it will
save them work. I shall want you to drive me into den
Haag in the morning. I am going to the hairdresser.'

'I only have my English licence with me,' said Cressida.

Jonkvrouw van Germert didn't bother to answer her.
'I shall want to leave at nine o'clock.' She got up. 'I hear
the car.'

Cressida remembered her manners and wished her
good night.

It was a pity that she didn't know more about being
a companion—she wasn't sure if eating in the kitchen

was one of the drawbacks but since she was hungry there wasn't much she could do about it. When her employer was in a better mood it might be possible to bring the subject up. Summoned by Corrie presently, she joined her and Cook at the kitchen table to find that they were as uneasy about the situation as she was. The food, though, was good and they both did their best to talk to her, indeed by the end of the meal the conversation, with the help of gestures and guesswork, was quite animated. Her offer to help clear the table was refused and Corrie pointed to the ceiling. 'Not good here,' she managed. 'You above.'

'Oh, Corrie, what a kind thing to say,' said Cressida warmly, and although they hadn't understood her words the meaning was clear. They both smiled widely and wished her, '*Wel te rusten.*'

She had two friends, she thought as she climbed into bed.

Dr van der Linus, his work finished at the hospital, let himself into his house in Leiden, to be greeted by Mies and the dogs and go to sit in his pleasant drawing-room. He had stayed longer at the hospital than he had expected and his plan to drive to den Haag and see Nicola no longer held any attraction for him, and in any case she wasn't expecting him back for another two days. Sitting by the fire, a drink in his hand and the dogs at his feet, he thought about Cressida. He had dissembled well enough; she plainly had no idea that he already knew where she was and had in fact arranged for her to be there in the first place. He would go and see her as soon as he had time to spare. She had looked not exactly sad when he had seen her across the street but certainly not happy, although when she had seen him her whole face had lit up. He would find out when next he saw her. He ate the delicious dinner Mies set before him and spent the rest of the evening in his study. He had a busy day ahead of him; Outpatients, a ward-round, private patients to see... He dismissed Cressida from his mind.

He had a few hours free on the afternoon following; just time enough to go and see Cressida. He supposed that he should take Nicola with him, and after lunch drove to den Haag. She greeted him with a surprise which concealed vexation. 'Aldrik—you weren't coming back until tomorrow.'

'I came back two days ago,' he told her, 'but I've been busier than usual. I'm free for a couple of hours, so I thought we might go to your aunt's and see how Miss Preece is getting on.'

Nicola answered too quickly. 'Oh, must we? Couldn't we go for a drive? She won't be expecting us...'

He gave her a thoughtful look. 'Well, it is a drive to Noordwijk-aan-Zee, albeit a short one, and there's no need to stand on ceremony.' He picked up a coat she had tossed down on a chair. 'Put this on and we'll go— I haven't all that much time to spare.'

He was a quiet man and calm but she knew that he had an inflexible will. There was no point in annoying him, besides she wasn't sure of him yet...

She hoped that Tante Clotilde would put on a show of treating the wretched English girl as though she were a treasured member of the household. A pity she hadn't had the time to telephone; if only her coat hadn't been lying there handy... It was no good worrying. She laid herself out to be charming, asking questions about his trip to France and pretending to be interested in the answers.

Corrie admitted them and showed them at once into the drawing-room where Jonkvrouw van Germert was lying on a sofa, leafing through a magazine. Taken unawares, she threw a look which boded no good to Corrie and got to her feet, her face wreathed in a hasty smile.

'Nicola, dear, how delightful, and Aldrik. Forgive me, but I was having a brief rest. This is quite a large house you know and there is more than enough for the servants to do—I help out when I can but I'm not strong and get quickly exhausted.'

A piece of nonsense which caused the doctor to lift his eyebrows a fraction. 'Surely Miss Preece is able to take the less important chores off your hands?' he asked mildly.

'Oh, of course,' gushed his hostess, 'such a good girl and so willing. Of course you would like to see her. Corrie shall fetch her for you.'

She tugged the bell rope by the fireplace and when Corrie came told her to fetch Miss Preece.

Corrie, who intended to stay in the house only until such time as she could find a better job, saw a chance to get some of her own back—she had broken a jug that morning and Jonkvrouw van Germert had told her its value would be taken out of her wages, which weren't generous to begin with.

'Certainly, *Mevrouw*, but you'll have to wait a while. Miss Preece is in the middle of turning out the pantry as you told her to.'

Jonkvrouw van Germert went puce and drew such a deep breath that her corsets creaked. 'Very well, but ask her to come as soon as she can.'

She turned to the doctor, standing by the window, looking out at the wintry garden. 'Such a dear girl, always suggesting ways to help. Quite invaluable in the house.'

He made a most non-committal reply and watched his companions' unease from under his lids, and, when Nicola began an animated conversation, joined in quite pleasantly.

It was ten minutes before Cressida joined them and Jonkvrouw van Germert said at once, 'Ah, there you are, my dear. I want you to meet my visitors—my niece, Nicola van Germert and Dr van der Linus.'

Cressida had gone faintly pink at the sight of the doctor and then pale but she shook Nicola's hand and murmured politely before offering a hand to him. He took it in his and said blandly. 'Oh, but Cressida and I know each other—we met several times in England and saw each other briefly in Leiden a couple of days ago.' He was aware of Nicola and her aunt exchanging glances and went on, 'I do hope you have settled down, Cressida, and are enjoying yourself.'

He was still holding her hand in his, aware that it was red and rough; the pantry was probably only one of the chores he suspected she was expected to undertake. 'You're happy?' he asked in a voice which expected an answer.

She said in a pleasant polite little voice, 'Yes, thank you, Doctor,' and withdrew her hand gently, giving him only the briefest of glances.

'Well, I'm sure she should be,' said Jonkvrouw van Germert in a rather too loud a voice. 'It isn't every girl who has a good job found for her. I hope you've thanked the doctor, Miss Preece, for it was he who asked me to employ you, you know; he knew that his grandmother could only have you for a few weeks—she took you in out of the kindness of her heart, isn't that so, Aldrik?'

The doctor remained perfectly calm; only his eyes gleamed under their lids. He said evenly, 'That is so, but one must also add that Cressida filled a much needed want with my Grandmother, just as I trust that she is doing here.'

Cressida's cheeks were a shade paler. 'I didn't know. I thought that Mrs Sefton... I'm very grateful to you, Doctor.'

Rage and humiliation sent the colour flying into her face, and her eyes flashed with temper. At that moment she hated everyone in the room, especially the doctor. She said clearly, 'And now, if you will excuse me, I'll go back and finish scrubbing out the pantry.'

Her exit, considering that she was a small, unassuming girl, was magnificently dignified.

CHAPTER FIVE

CRESSIDA closed the door with a deliberate quietness far more effective than a good slam, and the doctor's firm mouth twitched. He said suavely, 'I see that I have been at fault. Quite unwittingly I must have given you the impression that Cressida was a domestic worker, Jonkvrouw van Germert.' He glanced at Nicola. 'Did you think that, Nicola?'

'Oh, I really don't remember what you said. And anyway, why all the fuss? The girl's got a good home here and I'm sure Tante Clotilde is most considerate towards her. After all, she has to earn her living—one job must be as good as another.' She shrugged elegant shoulders. 'And there's no need to make a fuss about cleaning a pantry, surely...?'

'Have you ever cleaned a pantry?' enquired the doctor gently.

She made haste to change her tactics. 'No, you know I haven't, Aldrik, and I'm sorry if I'm being unkind. I'll come tomorrow and have a talk to her, shall I? And perhaps Tante Clotilde and I can rearrange her duties.' She added in a sympathetic voice, 'Of course the poor girl was upset, but I'm sure I can try to put things right. Will you leave it to me?' She smiled coaxingly. 'Women are so much better at that sort of thing than men.'

The doctor hesitated and then agreed. Nicola was right, of course; she would be able to smooth things over far better than he could, for one thing she could talk to her aunt with a good deal more frankness than he could, and, since Jonkvrouw van Germert expressed her concern and agreed that Cressida's duties should be considerably altered, he left with Nicola shortly afterwards. There was no sign of Cressida and on the whole he thought it best not to see her until things had been changed and she had settled down. All the same, he still neither liked nor completely trusted Jonkvrouw van Germert.

It was a matter he was forced to dismiss once he returned to the hospital, and, since he didn't get home until much later that evening, the remaining hours of which were taken up with walking the dogs, eating a delayed dinner and then dictating letters and notes into his Dictaphone until well after midnight, he shelved the problem until he had the leisure to solve it to his liking.

Nicola, on the other hand, had the leisure to review the situation thoroughly. It had been most unfortunate that Aldrik had returned home several days ahead of the expected date, and, worse, had met Cressida. The girl couldn't have complained to him, since he had said nothing, and he had been angry when her aunt had told Cressida that it was he who had arranged the job for her on the first instance. Nicola frowned; any other man would have lost his temper or at least demanded to know why the girl was being treated like a servant, but Aldrik had exhibited no sign of annoyance. She had known him for some time now and long since decided that she would marry him—he had a splendid home, more than enough money, and was already a name to be reckoned with in the medical profession. She didn't love him, but he was handsome, had beautiful manners and many friends. She had never known him to show anger but now she wasn't sure... Presently she reached for the phone and dialled her aunt's number.

The pantry had never been so clean; Cressida vented her temper upon its shelves and floor and emerged presently to tidy herself and present herself in the drawing-room for her daily task of writing out the shopping-list for her employer. She had missed the afternoon cup of tea served at half-past three o'clock although Corrie had brought her a cup of coffee, and, without speaking, helped her to put everything back in its place.

Jonkvrouw van Germert was still dangerously high-coloured and embarked on an involved excuse for her treatment of Cressida; she had never had a companion, she explained, and had no idea that Cressida expected to be treated as a guest in the house. 'And heaven knows that there is more than enough for you to do in the house and I cannot see why you should object to a little light housework—I felt quite ashamed before Dr van der Linus.'

Cressida, her good nature torn in shreds, said that she was glad to hear it. 'It is quite obvious that I took this job under a misapprehension. I thought at first that things would improve but each day you have treated me more like a servant and less like a companion. I think that we do not suit each other, *mevrouw*, and that it will be better if I leave.'

'No, no, there is no need for that, I'm sure that we can come to some amicable agreement, Miss Preece. At least let us wait until tomorrow when we shall both feel better able to discuss the matter.' She added with a touch of malice, 'It is a pity that you didn't know that it was Dr van der Linus who persuaded me to take you.'

To which Cressida made no reply and the rest of the evening was spent in an atmosphere of frigid politeness.

She was unpicking the muddle of her employer's knitting when Nicola arrived. She put it down at once and got up to leave the room but Nicola stopped her. 'No, sit down again, I've come to talk to both of you.' She exchanged a look with her aunt. 'We really must discuss things, mustn't we?'

Cressida didn't answer. She had no wish to discuss anything; she didn't like Nicola any more than she liked her aunt and Nicola had been very possessive towards the doctor. Surely he didn't intend to marry her? If so, he was both blind and bent on being unhappy for the rest of his life. Nicola, thought Cressida, was a young version of her own stepmother. He deserved better than that, although she hadn't forgiven him for deceiving her, however kindly his intentions had been.

Nicola made herself comfortable. 'Could we have some coffee?' she wanted to know. 'I missed lunch. Perhaps Miss Preece wouldn't mind going to the kitchen and asking Corrie to bring some here?'

Cressida put down the knitting. 'Yes, of course,' she kept her voice determinedly polite. She wanted to be out of the way while Nicola conferred with her aunt. She was right, of course; the moment she was out of the way, Nicola said urgently, 'Now, Tante Clotilde, leave the talking to me...'

Cressida came back and Corrie followed her presently with the coffee-tray and the three of them sat around drinking it and discussing the weather, the approach of St Nikolaas and Christmas, but soon Nicola put her coffee-cup down.

'Aldrik—Dr van der Linus—asked me to come and talk to you, Miss Preece. I'm afraid that you upset him yesterday. You see, he had gone to a great deal of trouble on your behalf, first persuading his grandmother—you didn't know that Lady Merrill was that?—to take you in under the guise of companion which she did while he sought for a permanent post for you. Of course he told me about you—we have no secrets—and I suggested that my aunt should employ you. He came here and discussed it with us both and was quite satisfied that it was just the kind of work you could do—you have no qualifications, have you? You can imagine how he feels at your show of ingratitude. He told me how much he pitied you and he has been to a good deal of trouble on your behalf. The least you can do is to show your real gratitude by doing your work without complaining.'

Cressida had listened without a sound to this speech. That she was boiling over with rage wasn't discernible; her ordinary face was composed even if it was pale, and when she spoke her voice was quiet and pleasant.

'Out of the frying-pan, into the fire,' she observed, and had the satisfaction of seeing the puzzlement on her companions' faces. 'I don't think there is anything we can say to each other, Juffrouw van Germert. You may have come with the best intentions, but I doubt it.' She put the knitting down, and set her cup and saucer on the tray. 'I'll leave you, if I may?' She looked at Jonkvrouw van Germert, whose formidable bosom was heaving quite alarmingly. 'I expect you would like to discuss me together.'

She went straight upstairs to her room, took her two cases from under the bed and packed her things, doing it neatly and unhurriedly, then changed into her warmest clothes, checked her handbag for money and passport, and, carrying her luggage, went downstairs. The drawing-room door was shut and she made no attempt to go there but went through the hall to the kitchen where she bade

an astonished Corrie and Cook goodbye and then, via
the back door, left the house.

It was bitterly cold and the cases were awkward, but,
carried along on a right royal rage, she hardly noticed
this. At the bus station she was lucky, for a bus was due
to leave within a few minutes, and she got herself on
board and sat, her head empty of thought, until it finally
reached Leiden. It was no distance to the station, she
bought a ticket to the Hoek and sat down on the platform
to wait for the train. The enormity of what she had done
was just beginning to penetrate her rage. There was no
going back; indeed, wild horses wouldn't have persuaded her to do that. To go back to England was the
obvious thing to do; luckily she had the best part of the
hundred pounds in her purse and she knew that a ferry
sailed from the Hoek at around midnight. It was a little
after five o'clock, she had ample time to get there and
at this time of year there should be no trouble getting a
ticket. Beyond that she wasn't going to think. She
couldn't go back to her home but surely she would find
work of some kind in London; anything would do until
she found her feet. She sat there, getting colder and
colder, not allowing herself to think of Dr van der Linus,
but, try as she might, her thoughts returned to him time
and again. She hadn't expected to meet him again but
she never would have forgotten him, she had thought of
him as a friend and she had confided in him. She could,
at a pinch, forgive him for deceiving her about his
grandmother, but to arrange for her to go to Holland
and to someone who disliked her and didn't want her
anyway was something she was unable to condone, and
to crown the whole unhappy business he had allowed
Nicola to take her to task for not being grateful. Worst
of all, though, he pitied her, in much the same way as

he had pitied the dog she had found. She would have liked to have a good cry but it was far too cold.

The train came presently and she found a seat, had a cup of the excellent coffee brought round, and, once they got to Rotterdam, found the train for the Hoek and got on board. She would have hours to wait there before she could go on board the ferry but she could sit in the café and have a bowl of soup in its noisy warmth.

The station at the Hoek was almost deserted; it was too early for the boat train and the local trains taking the workers home had dwindled to infrequency. The café was half full and she found a seat at a table by one of its windows and dawdled over a bowl of *Erwetensoep*, steaming hot pea soup, as thick as porridge and spiced with pork and sausage, and a roll, and then, leaving her cases in the care of the elderly couple who were sharing her table, she went to ask about a ticket. Its price made a serious hole in her money and a berth was out of the question, but she would be able to curl up on a bench somewhere, for the ship was half empty, she was told. She went back to the café and ordered a cup of coffee. The place was filling up now and in another half-hour or so the boat train would arrive and all the seats would be taken. The elderly couple were going on the ferry too, that much she had understood, but conversation was difficult, so they lapsed into a friendly silence and she was left to her thoughts.

She would have been missed by now, of course, and if Jonkvrouw van Germert had enquired, Corrie would have told her that Cressida had left with her luggage, but she didn't think anyone would try to fetch her back. Nicola would doubtless make up some story for the doctor's benefit and that would be the end of it. She fell to making plans—she would be in London early on the following morning, she could leave her luggage at the station, look up the nearest job centre in the phone book and get a job—any job—and then find a room, and if all else failed she would go to Castle Cary to Moggy. She was being optimistic, she knew, but domestic workers were in short supply and she would do anything while she looked around for the kind of work which she could do. The *Lady* magazine, she remembered, had been full of advertisements for help in the house and child-minders; she had only to buy a copy and find the nearest phone box ... Carried away on a cloud of optimism, she ordered another cup of coffee.

A train came in, not the boat train, although quite a few passengers got out and made for the exit to the ferry, and she wondered if it might be a good idea to go on board. It was warm in the café and she felt a certain comfort from the company of the nice elderly couple still sitting opposite her. She stared out of the wide window and gazed at the people hurrying to and fro and then glanced round the café. It had filled up, customers coming in as fast as those leaving; perhaps it would be a good idea to get on board before the boat train got in. Too late—it slid into the station silently and the platform was alive with passengers. There was still plenty of time before the ferry sailed and a good many of them crowded into the café, looking for seats and calling the waiters. Someone sat down in the empty seat beside her and she turned away from the window.

The doctor said quietly, 'Hello, Cressida.'

She was aware of the most intense delight at seeing him; she suppressed it at once and asked coldly, 'Why are you here? How did you know?'

'Corrie told me.' He was sitting very much at his ease and the elderly couple, gathering together their bags and parcels, gave him an enquiring look and then smiled when he spoke to them, nodding in a satisfied way before bidding him and Cressida goodbye.

'How kind of Corrie,' said Cressida, 'and now if you will be good enough to move I'll go on board the ferry.'

'Well, no, I think not. We might have a little talk. Would you like a cup of coffee?'

'I don't want to talk,' said Cressida bitterly, 'and I've had three cups of coffee. Oh, go away, do.'

She might just as well have asked an oak tree to uproot itself; the doctor's massive person remained sitting comfortably in his chair, and he had every appearance of a man who intended to stay where he was until he saw fit to move. She said in a despairing voice, 'Oh, please let me go—I've got my ticket...'

'Have you any money?' he asked so casually that she answered him at once. 'Oh, yes, the rest of the hundred pounds...' She stopped and turned to look at him. 'Mr Tims said—but it was you, wasn't it? You arranged it too, didn't you? Not content with pitying me, you had to...to...'

The doctor realised that this was the crux of the matter. 'What is all this nonsense about pitying you? Why should I? A great girl like you, quite able to earn your living once you had a leg up. Pity is the last thing I feel for you, my girl, and the quicker you disabuse yourself of that silly idea the better.'

He lifted a finger to a passing waiter, ordered a pot of tea and sat back, saying nothing until after the tea had been brought. 'Pour the tea, dear girl,' he suggested. 'It will improve your temper and then you can tell me exactly what has happened.'

'I don't want——' began Cressida crossly.

'Tut-tut, you have no reason to be peevish; a cup of tea can solve almost any problem for the British.'

So she poured the tea and drank most of hers until she put down the cup because the tears were running down her cheeks. She turned her head away, sniffed and put up a hand to wipe them away and had a large, very white handkerchief put into it. 'Wipe your face and have a good blow,' advised the doctor and when she had done so. 'Now start to talk, Cressida, and began at the beginning when you first arrived at Jonkvrouw van Germert's house.'

'Yes, all right, but first why did you send me there?'

'It hadn't been my intention, I had planned to send you to friends of mine in Friesland, but when Nicola suggested that her aunt would be glad to have you as a companion it seemed a better idea. I am a good deal in Leiden and I could have kept an eye on you.'

'Yes, well, I'm sure that Jonkvrouw van Germert was being kind.'

'Possibly.' The doctor's voice was dry. 'Why didn't you tell me you weren't happy when I saw you in Leiden?'

'I didn't know that you already knew that I was there, did I? I'd only been there a week and I thought—I thought I'd been rather clever to get a job so quickly after leaving Lady Merrill. You didn't tell me about her, either.' She gave a gulping breath and so he said carelessly,

'Why should I have done? Go on.'

There wasn't more much to tell and beyond telling him that Nicola had talked to her that afternoon she said nothing.

The doctor asked casually, 'So it was Nicola who told you that I found you work out of pity? I dare say that she pointed out your ingratitude, and told you that Lady

Merrill was my grandmother and hinted that I had discussed the whole matter with her, even suggested that I had sent her?'

'How did you know?'

'I didn't, but I know Nicola.' He added briskly, 'And now, having cleared up the matter, let us leave this place; the smell of food is horrendous and there are far too many people here.'

Cressida looked at the clock on the far wall. 'The ferry hasn't gone—they'll let me on if I hurry.'

'No, they won't, and don't think that they will let down the gangplank for a chit of a girl. You're coming back with me.'

'I'm not. I refuse. I'd rather die.'

'Don't be dramatic. You're coming back with me and my housekeeper will put you to bed and fuss over you and in the morning I shall drive you up to Friesland to some friends of mine and you'll stay with them until we find you the perfect job.'

'I bought my ticket.'

'We can get a refund. Come along now, I've had a long day.'

He picked up her cases and walked out of the station to the car, put the cases in the boot and stowed her in the front seat. 'Hungry?' he asked as he started the car.

'Yes.'

'We'll soon be home.' He didn't speak again and she was left with her thoughts and very muddled they were.

The Bentley made light of the journey. They were in Leiden while she was still sorting out her problems and presently the doctor stopped in a pleasant narrow street lined with old gabled houses and got out, opened her door and led her across the narrow cobbled pavement and up double steps to a handsome door with a fanlight over it. He unlocked it and pushed her gently before him just as Mies came from the kitchen.

Cressida stood in the hall, his arm around her shoulders, listening to him talking to his housekeeper, who presently clucked in a motherly fashion and led her away and up a charming little staircase to a pretty bedroom where she took Cressida's coat from her, still clucking, and opened the door to a small and exquisitely fitted bathroom and left her.

Cressida looked around her. The bed looked inviting; to fall into it and go to sleep at once was a tempting idea. Instead she went to look at herself in the triple mirror on the delicate little table under the window. She was horrified at what she saw; a tear-stained face, not over-clean, hair all over the place and a pink nose. She washed and combed her hair and wondered what to do next. Should she go downstairs or was she supposed to go to bed? She had no clothes until someone brought her cases. She opened the door cautiously and peered down the stairs.

The doctor was in the hall and both the dogs were with him. 'Come on down if you're ready,' he invited. 'Mies is putting supper on the table—you said you were hungry.' When she reached the bottom of the stairs he asked, 'What do you think of Caesar? This is Mabel, rather large but as mild as a lamb.'

His manner was brisk, like that, she supposed, of an elder brother taking dutiful care of a younger sister, and exactly what was needed to reassure her, as the doctor very well knew.

'In here,' he invited and opened a door. The room was of a good size with panelled walls and an ornate plaster ceiling from which hung a brass candelabrum. The furniture was old and beautifully cared for and the oval table had been laid with a damask cloth and shining silver and glass.

'But it's past midnight,' said Cressida. 'Who's going to clear away and wash up?'

'Mies has help in the mornings; the two girls who come will clear away and tidy things up.'

Mies came in then with a tureen of soup and said something, and he made a reply which made her smile broadly as she answered him. 'Mies says she will go to bed when you do and you are to enjoy your supper.'

The soup smelled delicious and tasted even better, Cressida was hungry, she polished off the soup, the cheese souffle which followed and the crème brulée which rounded off their meal, and then, mindful of the lateness of the hour, refused coffee and asked if she might go to bed.

The doctor bade her goodnight, handed her over to Mies and went to his study to finish the work he had been doing when Corrie had telephoned. The dogs went with him and he sat at his desk with them beside him, deep in thought. It was quite some time before he bestirred himself, and, with a sigh, picked up his pen.

As for Cressida, finding that someone had taken her cases to her room and unpacked what she might need for the night, she sank into a hot bath, only half awake, and then tumbled into bed. There was too much to think about all at once; sensibly she closed her eyes and went to sleep.

A stout girl with a rosy face and a broad smile wakened her with a small tea-tray, drew back the curtains, revealing a grey sky and a heavy frost, and then went away again. Cressida drank her tea, hopped out of bed and ran the bath. She had no idea what was to happen next but it seemed sense to get dressed and be ready for whatever transpired.

The doctor came out of his study with the dogs as she reached the hall. His good morning was friendly and decidedly brisk. 'Breakfast and then we'll be off. We are expected for lunch.'

Cressida found her voice. 'Yes, that's all very well, but where and what happens to me when we get there? It's really very kind of you to bother about me, but I've still got my ticket...'

He swept her into the dining-room and pulled out a chair. She sat down because it seemed the only thing to do; besides she was hungry and her eyes had caught a basket of delicious croissants on the table. Eggs too, and a sizeable dish of ham as well as elegant silver-topped glass jars filled with marmalade and jam. Mies came in with a silver coffee-pot, beaming and nodding. '*Smakelijk eten,*' she said.

Cressida, wrinkling her nose at the heavenly smell of coffee, said a polite, '*Dank U,*' reflecting that she was going to enjoy every crumb of her meal.

The doctor had seated himself at the head of the table, the dogs on either side. 'Perhaps you would rather have tea?' he said.

'Oh, no, thank you. Do you want me to pour?'

'Please. Try one of these croissants.' He passed the basket, the elaborate silver egg stand and the salt and pepper and then enquired as to whether she had slept well.

'Yes, it was a lovely comfy bed. I meant to stay awake and think but I was rather tired. Could we please talk, Dr van der Linus? There really is no need to go all the way to Friesland. I'm sure I can get work if I go back to England.'

He helped himself to ham. 'What as?'

'Well, as a companion, I suppose...' The memory of Jonkvrouw van Germert was a bit daunting but surely not all employers were like her?

He passed his cup for more coffee. 'Let us strike a bargain. Come with me to Friesland this morning and if you don't like the idea of finding work there I will personally put you on the ferry for England.'

She bit into a croissant. If she went back to England she would never see him again, on the other hand since she had chosen to make her way in the world that was a matter of little importance. The wretched Nicola would get round him and he would forgive her and marry her and be unhappy ever after...

'You can have ten minutes,' said the doctor in a no-nonsense voice, 'and bring everything with you.'

She swallowed her coffee and started up the stairs and then dawdled when she heard him say, 'Ah, Nicola,' as he answered the ringing phone. It was a pity that her knowledge of Dutch was so sparse and there was nothing to tell from is voice.

Mies saw them on their way with a good hearty handshake and what Cressida took to be kindly advice. The dogs, on the rugs on the back seat, settled down, and the doctor drove off.

'Shouldn't you be at the hospital?' asked Cressida.

'Occasionally I take a day off.' He took the road through Alkmaar and over the Afsluitdijk and she found so much to see that conversation wasn't really necessary. They were nearing Leeuwarden when the doctor said, 'These friends of mine—the van der Bronses, Tyco and Charity—they've been married just over a year, she's expecting a baby in a couple of months, there are two little girls who are from his first marriage, Teile and Letizia—they're twins and they adore Charity.'

'They don't mind having me like this at a moment's notice?'

'They're pleased. They haven't been living in Friesland very long; Tyco's father decided to sell his business and move into a villa he owns just outside Sneek, not too far away, and Tyco took over his big house. He's consultant at Leeuwarden and goes to Amsterdam fairly regularly. He's a very good surgeon. We were at medical school together.'

'Do you live near here?'

'Yes. North of Dokkum, a few miles from the Wadenzee.' He offered no more information and she didn't like to ask questions; there was, she reflected briefly, no future in their acquaintance.

Half an hour later he was stopping before the van der Brons home, a large country house set in a pleasant small park with open country all around. Nothing could have been warmer than the welcome Cressida received. She had been feeling incredibly nervous of meeting the doctor's friends but at the first sight of them she knew that she had been needlessly so. Mr van der Brons, as large a man as the doctor, had a kind face and twinkling eyes, he was handsome too which made it all the more surprising that his wife was as ordinary to look at as Cressida herself. True, she was wearing the kind of clothes Cressida envied at first look, and she was beautifully made up, but she was still plain. Cressida took instant comfort from that fact.

The doctor kissed his hostess soundly, shook his friend by the hand and introduced Cressida.

'Come in,' said Charity, 'the girls are longing to see you. Bring the dogs, Aldrik. Samson will be pleased; they can have a good run after lunch.'

They all went indoors and the doctor said, 'I must go back this afternoon—a clinic at four o'clock and I must call in at home on the way.'

'Come upstairs and see your room?' invited Charity, 'I'm so glad you could come, I don't get out a great deal.' She patted the elegant drapery over her tummy. 'We can have a good gossip.'

'You're very kind to have me. I wanted to go back to England but Dr van der Linus wouldn't let me.'

'Quite right, too.' Charity opened a door in the gallery at the top of the staircase. 'Here we are, someone will unpack for you while we're having lunch and while the men take the children and dogs for a walk we'll get to know each other.' She opened the door again. 'Come down when you're ready—we'll look out for you.'

Cressida, left to herself, explored the bedroom and the bathroom beyond, looked out of the window and then did her face and hair. It was rather like being in a dream, she reflected, and she supposed that sooner or later someone would tell her what was to happen next. Was she to stay here for one night? Was there a suitable job waiting for her? Or was she to stay longer and rely on local advertisements or agencies, and why had the doctor brought her all this way, as far away from the ferry as possible, or almost?

No way was she going to get the answers to her problems, not for the moment at any rate; they were waiting for her in the drawing-room and the two little girls were there too, and over drinks and lunch the talk never once touched on herself, but after the meal, when the children went to get their outdoor things and Charity went with them, Cressida found herself beside the doctor while Mr van der Brons was telephoning.

'I really must know what's going to happen to me,' she hissed at him. 'I can't stay here, I simply can't, you must tell me.'

He smiled down at her, very large and very calm. 'Charity will explain while we're out, and if when we get back you still want to go back to England I'll run you back to Leiden and put you on the train.'

He patted her shoulder and wandered away to where the others were waiting in the hall. She watched him go, feeling frustrated; she hadn't had the chance to say half the things which were on her mind.

Charity came back into the room. 'I'm going to put my feet up,' she said cheerfully, 'curl up in a chair and we can have a good gossip.'

Cressida curled up. 'Look,' she began, 'I'm most grateful to you and your husband for having me but I can't get Dr van der Linus to tell me anything...'

'Men can be tiresome,' observed Charity. 'They arrange things and expect everyone else, especially wives, to know all about it. Did he mention the ter Beemstras? No? Well, they live a few miles from here, youngish, six children and desperate for someone to help with them. You see, the idea of six is a bit daunting, isn't it? But it's not like that at all. The three eldest are at school all day—boys, the twins are five years old and the littlest one is three. I rather think that Aldrik thought you might like to take them on. Actually, he had them in mind when he came back to Holland, but Nicola persuaded him that you would be happier with her aunt.'

She rearranged a cushion to her satisfaction. 'If I had known I would have warned him—I've met Jonkvrouw van Germert once and that was once too often, and I can't stand Nicola, she's got her claws into Aldrik. You can't think how pleased I was when he phoned to say he was bringing you to us.' She beamed at Cressida. 'If you like the idea I'll get Beatrix ter Beemstra to come over and talk to you. They're a happy family and the house is nice and they'll be generous with a salary.' She added in her friendly way, 'It would be lovely to have you not too far away; you could pop over for coffee or lunch or something. The twins get on well with ours and the baby's a darling. Now I'm going to take a nap while you think about it.'

She closed her eyes and Cressida, with no chance to say a word, set about considering her situation. The idea of six children didn't daunt her; she liked them and she thought that she would like Friesland with its wide horizons and endless fields, and, although she told herself that it would make no difference, she might see the doctor from time to time. She liked Charity and Tyco and the twins and perhaps the ter Beemstras would like her too and she could settle down with them. If she went back to England she would be going to unknown people, even if she were lucky enough to find a job quickly .

Charity's soft voice broke into her thoughts. 'Would you like to meet Beatrix ter Beemstra? Just to talk about it . . .'

Cressida took a deep breath. 'Yes, please, if you think I'd do.'

Charity went over to the side-table by one of the windows and lifted the receiver as the door opened and the men, children and dogs came in. The doctor went straight to Cressida. 'I'm leaving in a few minutes.' He glanced across at Charity. 'Are you getting fixed up with the ter Beemstras?' And when she nodded he said, 'Good, I think you'll be happy with them. I'm sorry

CHAPTER SIX

STANDING in the porch with her new-found friends around her, Cressida wondered if she would ever see the doctor again. The Bentley disappeared into the gathering dusk and they went back to the drawing-room to have tea and then play Monopoly with the twins until it was their bedtime.

Charity went upstairs presently to tuck them up for the night and Tyco, sitting opposite Cressida, said in his kind way, 'I think you'll like the ter Beemstras, they're good friends of ours, but if anything bothers you don't hesitate to let us know. I promised Aldrik that I would keep an eye on you.'

'Thank you very much. I'm sure I'll be happy with your friends.' She hesitated. 'I didn't like to ask Dr van der Linus but I do hope that I haven't been the cause of any—any difference between him and Juffrouw van Germert.'

'I can safely reassure you about that.' He smiled at her and got up as Charity came back into the room. 'I believe he intends to see her this evening.'

'Oh, good, I'm glad,' said Cressida, who didn't feel glad at all.

Sitting between them presently, eating delicious food with Jolly, the butler, hovering benignly in the background, Cressida felt happy for the first time in days— well, almost happy; the thought that she had seen the doctor for the last time was ever present in the back of her mind. Even if he came to see the van der Bronses, he was hardly likely to see her. She wondered just where he lived and asked Charity.

'Oh, not far away—the other side of Dokkum, about ten miles from here. It's rather out of the way, though. He loves it, but Nicola hates it. He has a house in Leiden though—you've been there—handy for him, for he goes to and fro a good deal. I suppose he'll be there for Christmas; his father died a few years ago and his mother is on a long visit to one of his sisters. He has another sister with children, I dare say they'll be with him as well as aunts and cousins. Oh, and Nicola, wrapped in furs and looking gorgeous.'

Her husband laughed gently. 'I hate to disagree with you, my love, but I believe Aldrik will be in England for Christmas—with Lady Merrill. He'll be back here for New Year.'

That, thought Cressida vulgarly, will be one in the eye for Nicola, but she was instantly sobered by the thought that probably Nicola would go with him.

She went to bed presently, convinced that she would lie awake most of the night, there was so much on her mind, but of course she was asleep as soon as her head was on the pillow.

The little girls were driven to school by their father on his way to his consulting rooms in Leeuwarden and Mevrouw ter Beemstra wouldn't arrive until just after ten o'clock for coffee; Charity took Cressida round the house and never mentioned Aldrik once. Cressida didn't know whether to be pleased about this or not. On the one hand the sooner she thought less about him the better, but, on the other, it would be nice to know more about him.

Beatrix ter Beemstra was a tall good-looking young woman of five and thirty with corn-coloured hair and

very blue eyes. She spoke good English and she had a
happy face. She shook hands with Cressida and gave her
a frank look. 'Six,' she said and laughed, 'six children—
we think they're wonderful, but that's because they're
ours. Will you come and give us a try? The eldest boys
are at school all day, there are three—my husband takes
them into Leeuwarden each morning, then there are two
little girls, five years old, twins, and Lucia, she's just
three years old—we call her Baby.'

Jolly brought in the coffee and the three of them sat
for an hour while she explained just what Cressida would
have to do. 'If you find it too much just say so. We still
have Nanny with us, she looks after Lucia to a large
extent and of course you won't be expected to do anything but look after the children, speak English to them
and be prepared to play with them and go for walks and
so on.' She smiled at Cressida. 'Would you like to try?'

Cressida liked her and she would be kept busy enough
not to have time to repine. Besides, the wages were really
very generous; she would be able to save a good deal,
gain experience, learn to speak Dutch, and when she was
ready she could return to England. She wasn't sure what
she would do when she got there but it was something
to aim for.

She said now, 'Yes, please, if you're sure I'll do. When
would you like me to start?'

Charity said quickly, 'Oh, please let us have her here
for a day or two, just until after Sint Nikolaas—it's only
two days away.'

Beatrix ter Beemstra agreed readily enough. 'That will
give you a couple of weeks before the boys start their
holidays. The twins start school in the New Year, though
we shan't send them until half-term, but of course they'll
all be home for Christmas.' She added a little anxiously,

'You like walking and cycling? Good—there's a bike for you—the children go for miles.'

She got up to go. 'I hope you'll be very happy with us. We shall do our best to make you feel at home.'

She shook Cressida's hand, kissed Charity and drove off in her Mini.

'Tomorrow,' said Charity comfortably, 'we shall go into Leeuwarden and shop for Sint Nikolaas—he comes to the village and we all go to meet him. The children love it; he hands out oranges and sweets and they put their shoes in the hearth and he leaves something in them. Come to the kitchen with me, I must talk to Mrs Jolly about dinner this evening. Tyco will be home for lunch and so will the children.'

If it hadn't been for the persistent niggling thought at the back of her mind about Aldrik, Cressida would have been completely happy. She felt at home—and not only with the van der Bronses, but with the countryside and the quiet. Leeuwarden wasn't all that far away but here at the nice old house there were only fields, empty of cows now that it was winter, and half-frozen canals, and not far away, shielded by bare trees, the tiled roofs of the village, dominated by its church. She was going to be happy here, she told herself resolutely, and, indeed, for the rest of that day, in the friendly company of the two little girls and Charity and Tyco, she was.

Charity had a little car of her own, another Mini, and Cressida drove them both into Leeuwarden the following morning. It was a pleasant city with some charming old buildings; she promised herself that she would explore it on one of her free days later on and following Charity she went to the shops.

She had the rest of the hundred pounds in her purse and since she would be earning quite handsomely in the

near future she bought chocolate letters for Teile and
Letizia, and, at Charity's insistence, some thick woollen
tights for herself. 'If you're to go cycling with the children
you'll need them,' said Charity. 'Did that woman pay
you?'

'Well, no, but I was there less than a fortnight. I'd
rather not bother about it. I've enough money until I
get paid.'

They went back presently, laden with their parcels:
bracelets for the twins, a scarf for Mrs Jolly, a box of
cigars for Jolly and a rich silk tie for Tyco, and added
to these boxes of sweets and crystallised fruit, and a
magnificent chocolate cake, to be met by the children
and Tyco and presently eat lunch. Listening to the happy
chatter all around her, Cressida reflected that it was a
good thing that she would soon be gone; she wasn't
serious but she was filled with a wistful longing to be
happy as the van der Bronses were happy, and, since
that seemed highly unlikely, the sooner she got herself
settled with plenty to fill her days and her thoughts the
better it would be.

Tyco came home early on the following day and drove
them all to the village to watch Sint Nikolaas, on his
splendid white horse with Zwarte Piet beside him, enter
the village and gravely acknowledge the greetings of
everyone there, and then proceed to the village hall where
he delivered a homily to the children and then read each
child's name from the list in his hand. One by one they
went to him to be asked if they had been good, and,
since legend had it that Zwarte Piet would pop any
naughty child into the sack he carried on his shoulder,
they were all good, running back triumphantly to their
mothers and fathers clutching their orange and bag of
sweets. Teile and Letizia went in their turn and then

joined in the singing as the *sint* departed, mounted his horse and rode away. Cressida had enjoyed the simple ceremony but there were still treats in store, she was assured by the children as they drove back to the house, and sure enough they had barely finished tea when there was a thunderous knock on the house door and Jolly came in with a small sack. Sint Nikolaas, he informed them, had called only a few moments ago and left it, at the same time reminding the children that they must put their shoes out when they went to bed with a wisp of hay in them for his horse.

Mr van der Brons opened the sack. The twins first, of course; several gaily wrapped boxes for each of them and then gifts for Jolly and Mrs Jolly, and a package for Cressida which she was made to open at once. Gloves, soft leather, lined with silk and elegant as well as warm. 'Thank the *sint*,' said Charity, 'we all have to.'

Charity was next, and under the wrappings a small velvet box containing a pair of diamond earrings. She thanked the *sint* and smiled at Tyco, looking so happy that Cressida felt a lump in her throat. Tyco was last. He admired the tie, praised the *sint*'s good taste and vowed that he would wear it that very evening, which was the signal for Charity to mention that a few friends would be coming in to dinner. 'I shall wear my earrings,' she said happily. 'We had better go and tidy ourselves before they get here.' She glanced at her husband. 'Do you suppose Sint Nikolaas would agree to the girls staying up for dinner?'

'There will be so many of us that two more won't be noticed, darling. Best behaviour, of course; Oma and Opa will be here.'

They went their separate ways and Cressida got into the grey dress which was hardly festive but would do at a pinch, she supposed. She did her face with care and took pains with her hair, all the while wondering what the doctor was doing.

Dr van der Linus was at the hospital in Leiden, using all his skill to keep alive an elderly man who had collapsed in the street that afternoon. He should by rights have been in den Haag at Nicola's home, where her parents were giving a dinner party, but he had asked that someone should telephone them and explain that he would be very late or possibly not get there at all. After that he hadn't thought about it at all; he was wholly engrossed in his patient. The young houseman who had sent his message had been shocked by the petulance of the voice which answered him. He was to tell Dr van der Linus that his absence was most inconvenient and that he had been very inconsiderate. The receiver had been slammed down before the young man could say anything more. He went back and said merely that he had given the doctor's message; if the owner of the voice was the young lady the hospital grapevine alleged he would eventually marry then he for one was convinced that she wouldn't do at all; the chief was liked and respected and unfailingly patient and courteous with the most trying of medical students. He deserved better.

The doctor, going home at last, ate his solitary supper, sent Mies to her bed and took the dogs walking. It was very cold with a moon doing its best to escape the clouds and he walked briskly. He was tired but satisfied that the man had a good chance of recovery. He didn't think about Nicola at all, only as he let himself and the dogs into his house he wondered what Cressida was doing. 'But of course she will be in bed and asleep,' he muttered to himself and Caesar as they followed Mabel in the kitchen.

She was certainly in bed, but she wasn't sleeping, she was thinking about him.

She had had a happy evening. Tyco had a large family, parents and brothers and sisters, and there had been children too. Dinner had been on a grand scale; Cressida reflected with pleasure upon the delights of lobster bisque, roast pheasant, champagne sorbets and a magnificent ice pudding. They had drunk champagne too and afterwards there had been friends calling in for drinks. It was a pity that the doctor couldn't have been there too but she supposed that he would spend his spare time with Nicola. As long as he was happy, she thought sleepily, and nodded off. She woke in the night, sad and lonely, feeling as though she had lost something dear to her. That was nonsense, she told herself; perhaps it was a forgotten dream which had given her that bereft feeling and the small hours of the morning were notorious for their gloom. She slept again uneasily and got up to finish her packing. The ter Beemstras would be coming for her soon after ten.

She said goodbye to Tyco at breakfast, kissed the twins and promised that she would come and see them as soon as she could, then sat down again to have another cup of coffee with Charity.

'We shall see you at Christmas, if not before. We may be a little out of the way here but we are quite social. I do hope Aldrik comes up to Janslum—Tyco says he'll be in England with his grandmother but he's sure to be back for New Year. He goes to and fro the way anyone would catch a bus, if you see what I mean.'

Mevrouw ter Beemstra was punctual; Cressida, her eyes said with hidden reluctance, got into the car of her new employer, and was immediately much by that lady's profound relief. 'I've been so afraid you might have second thoughts,' she said. 'It's the six children—they put people off, you know...'

Cressida reassured her. 'I don't know much about it,' she said, 'but I should have thought that several children must be a lot easier to amuse than one, and they're never lonely...'

Their drive was a short one and the house when they reached it looked pleasant. Smaller than the van der Bronses', but with a good deal of ground around it. The door was flung open as they got out and children and dogs came tumbling out to greet them.

'The boys have stayed at home especially to greet you,' said Mevrouw ter Beemstra, 'and my husband also will come for lunch and take them back with him for afternoon school. Now I will tell you their names; Willum, our eldest son, Jacobus, Friso, and the twins Sepke and Galske and the baby Lucia. They speak a little English and I hope you will speak English to them at all times, Miss Preece—must I call you that?'

'I'd like it if you would call me Cressida and I'd like the children to call me that too. Miss Preece makes me sound like an elderly governess.'

She shook hands with the children in turn, first Willum, twelve years old, rather a solemn boy, and, she suspected, very conscious that he was the eldest. Jacobus, two years younger, had a round jolly face and a thatch of unruly gold hair and Friso, eight years old, was very like him. The twins were sturdy with bright blue eyes and blonde pigtails and looked older than their five years, they each held a hand of Lucia, a cherub with golden curls who, when it came to her turn, put up her face to be kissed and shouted, '*Dag, Cressy!*' and burst into giggles.

'We call you Cressy,' said Willum, and they all nodded, and when their mother remonstrated Cressida said, 'Oh, I think that's a splendid idea, so much easier than Cressida, isn't it?'

They all went into the house then, through the tiled hall and into a lofty room with windows at each end, very comfortably furnished and cluttered with books and toys. *Mevrouw* swept a pile of magazines off a roomy sofa and bade Cressida sit down. 'The room is not tidy, but the playroom and nursery are at the top of the house and it is too far, you understand? But now that you are here there will be someone to be with them. The boys are old enough to go cycling together and Willum has his own room now, but the little girls may not go out alone.'

She sat down beside Cressida. 'Let us have coffee and then you shall see your room and the house and meet everyone.'

A tall bony woman brought the coffee and Mevrouw ter Beemstra said, 'This is Leike, she speaks no English but she will help you all she can.'

Cressida shook hands and Leike smiled from a fairly stern face. Looking around her, Cressida had that nice warm feeling that she was going to be happy.

Mijnheer ter Beemstra came home for lunch. A large man, thick-set, and a good deal older than his wife with a rugged good-humoured face. His children fell upon him, all talking at once, as his wife introduced Cressida. He shook hands, smiling broadly. 'We are glad to welcome you, Miss Preece, and we hope that you will be happy with us; you will also be busy...'

Sitting up in bed, much later, Cressida paused in writing a letter to Moggy to review her day. It had been full, not a minute wasted from the moment when she had been led upstairs to her room, a small cosy place comfortably furnished and with a view out over the wide fields beyond the grounds, then, accompanied by all six children, she had been taken on a tour of the house. The children had come to show her everything and they had rooms close to hers, and at the end of a long passage there was a big playroom and beside it a smaller room, used as a nursery for Baby. Here she had met Lucia's nurse, elderly, her beady eyes studying Cressida with guarded politeness. Of course, Cressida had thought, she was afraid that Cressida was going to usurp her position, something she had no intention of doing. She had contrived to let the nurse understand this with the help of Willum, who'd laboured away doing his best to translate for her. It had been a relief to see the nurse relax presently.

English was to be spoken at meals; lunch had been a hilarious affair with her encouraging and correcting and offering, rather diffidently, to improve upon an accent. Afterwards, walking down to the village to buy stamps at the little post office, accompanied by everyone except Lucia, she had been teased into trying her Dutch. Which, Willum solemnly told her, was very bad.

At the end of the day, getting them to bed had been a major operation, so that when she went downstairs finally and Mevrouw ter Beemstra suggested that she might like to go to bed herself she was glad to go. Perhaps, she reflected, it would be a good idea if she did that every evening, she could always plead letters to write and probably once she had got settled in there would be odd jobs of mending and so on which she could do in the playroom.

She punched her pillows into greater comfort and thought about her free day. It was to be Thursday be-

cause the girls went to dancing class in the afternoon
and the boys had fencing lessons; she could, if she
wished, go in to Leeuwarden with Mijnheer ter Beemstra
after breakfast and return when she liked; there was a
bus which went through the village in the evening, but
if she missed it, she only had to telephone and she would
be fetched. The last weekend of each month was to be
hers too. She could stay in the house if she wished and
go somewhere each day or she could go away for the
weekend. 'I belive that Charity will love to have you,'
said Mevrouw ter Beemstra kindly.

She would go to Leeuwarden, she decided, and have
a good look round, and since Christmas was only a
couple of weeks away she would buy small gifts and one
or two cards—for Moggy and her sister and Mr Tims,
Charity and Tyco and Cook and Dr van der Linus. She
wondered what he was doing, picturing him in Nicola's
company. She allowed her imagination to run away with
her; Nicola would be quite exquisitely dressed and
looking prettier than ever, trilling her tinkling laugh,
asking him sympathetically something about his day's
work, making him smile. Cressida was suddenly consumed with a profound dislike of the girl; she was all
wrong for the doctor and he was extremely silly not to
see that for himself. Well, let him cook his own goose,
she muttered, and picked up her pen once more and
wrote several pages of cheerful news to Moggy.

She slipped into the life of the household quickly, helped
by Mevrouw ter Beemstra's kindly hints and the en-
thusiastic encouragement of the children. Her days were
busy, for there were always children around, with the
constant need to speak English and whenever possible
have it read to them. She set herself, within the first day

or so, to learn as many Dutch words as possible, and it was surprising how easy it was to understand the children; committed to speak English with all of them, she didn't venture to try them out, but she listened while she was with them and boldly tried out the few words she had understood on the maid and the elderly cook in the kitchen, quite undeterred when one of them failed to understand her.

Her duties, away from the children, were light—she made her bed but no one expected her to do any household chores although there was plenty of mending and occasional ironing to do for the children—but her days were full enough, keeping six children occupied while they were not at school. She made sure that they bathed, washing their flaxen hair, putting plasters on grazed knees, helping them with their English lessons. The two elder boys brought home a good deal of homework and since she had a smattering of Latin grammar and knew something of geometry and algebra she rose in their regard. It was with Friso and the two girls that she had most contact; their English was sketchy and they were at an age when learning was a bore anyway. All the same, by the end of the first week she had devised several ways of making it more attractive to them, taking them for walks or cycle rides, getting them to tell her names of the trees and flowers and everything else in sight and then repeating everything in English. Baby, of course, was no trouble at all; her nurse relinquished her from time to time and Cressida soon had her prattling away, quite happy to speak any language anyone should choose to teach her.

The week flew by and on the Wednesday evening Charity telephoned to invite her over for her free day. 'I'll come and fetch you,' she offered, 'and Tyco shall take you back after dinner. I'll be there about half-past nine so mind you're ready.'

The weather had turned fine with a pale blue sky, a searing cold wind and thin ice on the canals. Cressida, wrapped in her winter coat and wearing the woolly hat and scarf she had bought in Leiden, bade the ter Beemstras goodbye and got into Charity's car.

'Ought you to be driving?' she asked as they started off.

'I promised Tyco this morning that I won't take the car out again until after I've had the baby. He's fussy...' Somehow it sounded high praise.

'I can drive you,' said Cressida.

'Oh, thanks—we'll go shopping together. I love Christmas, don't you?' Charity overtook a farm tractor with caution. 'Well, how do you like the job? The ter Beemstras are delighted with you—Beatrix told me when I phoned yesterday.'

'It's marvellous. They're so kind and I don't have to do any housework.'

'I should hope not. I can't think what came over Aldrik, letting you go to that horrible woman.'

'Well, if he's in love with Nicola and she suggested it I suppose he thought it would be all right.'

'He's not in love with her, though. She's fastened on to him and he's too busy and wrapped up in his work to do anything about it.'

Somehow this piece of news cheered Cressida up. 'Oh, do you think so?' She would have liked to have pursued the matter but they had arrived at Charity's home and Jolly came out to drive the car round to the garage for her and beg them to hurry inside. 'Mrs Jolly's got the coffee ready, *Mevrouw*, and there's a good fire in the small sitting-room.'

There was a great deal to talk about; Christmas—and things to do with the children during the school holidays. 'Tyco's family come over for Christmas and of course we'll have a party. You'll come...?'

'Will I? Supposing the ter Beemstras want to go out? There'll be the children to mind.'

'They'll come too. Baby's nurse will come and our housemaid is marvellous with children and we can pop in and out. They have a room to play in and their own food. Tyco says they've always done it, and they come and join the grown-ups when the presents are handed out.'

'Won't it be a bit much for you?'

Charity poured more coffee. 'Me? No, no. Besides, there's you and Tyco's sisters and Mrs Jolly and the ter Beemstras. It'll be great fun.'

She glanced at Cressida. 'I'm sorry Aldrik won't be here. He's splendid with children.' She sighed. 'I suppose if Nicola succeeds in getting him to marry her she'll have lots of nasty little Nicolas...'

'She doesn't look as if she would like even one.'

'That won't suit Aldrik; he told me once that he would like a large family when he married.'

She got up. 'Come and see the nursery, it's all ready—the girls helped me and we've had such fun. Tyco keeps bringing home teddy bears and rattles...'

They spent a pleasant hour while Cressida admired everything before going to Charity's bedroom to go through her wardrobe and try on her hats. They went downstairs for lunch presently and just as they reached the hall the front door opened and Tyco and Aldrik came in.

'Hello, darling—Cressida too.' Tyco kissed his wife, 'Aldrik's on the way to Janslum; I've brought him home for lunch.'

Charity lifted her face for Aldrik's kiss. 'How very nice, and here's Cressida, spending her day off with us.'

Cressida offered a hand and smiled up at him, aware of a deep delight at seeing him again. He took it in his own large one and bent and kissed her cheek. 'This is an unexpected pleasure,' he told her, and Tyco, his arm around his wife, winked at her. 'I have been wondering how you have been getting on.'

Cressida had gone rather pink. She had enjoyed the kiss but it mustn't be allowed to go to her head, she reflected. 'I'm very happy,' she told him. 'Everyone is kind and the children are dears.'

She came to a halt, wishing very much to tell him every detail of her days. That would bore him, she thought, so instead she asked politely, 'I hope you haven't been too busy?'

The doctor, who had been out of his bed for most of the night after a long day at Amsterdam Hospital, assured her that he hadn't been at all busy, and Tyco suggested that they might all go to the drawing-room and have a drink before lunch.

'Teile and Letizia will be here in a few minutes,' said Charity. 'Mrs Jolly's gone to fetch them.'

Lunch was a very cheerful meal; Christmas was near enough for it to be the main topic of conversation and the twins could talk of nothing else, but presently Tyco said, 'Well, I've a couple of patients to see and I said I'd look in at the hospital. I'll drop these two off as I go. Tell Jolly to fetch them after school, my love, will you? I'll be back about five o'clock.' The children went to get their outdoor things and as Charity got up too he said, 'And you'll put your feet up, darling.'

'While you're doing that,' said Aldrik casually, 'I'll take Cressida over to Janslum. It will give her the chance to see something of the country.'

Charity was buttoning the twins into their coats and Cressida got up to help her. She said over her shoulder, 'It's most kind of you, Doctor, but I shall be very happy to stay here and read—or something—while Charity rests.'

'Oh, I'm not being kind.' He spoke carelessly. 'Tyske—my housekeeper—has made *speculaas* and I won't be able to eat all of them; besides, the dogs are there—I brought them up with me last night.'

He added briskly, 'Caesar is very fit, I thought you might like to see him—and Mabel, of course.'

'Well, yes, I would—thank you. I'll come...'

'You'll enjoy the drive,' said Charity, 'and you'll both come back here for dinner—seven o'clock, because Cressida wants to be back by ten o'clock.' She added, 'And bring the dogs, Aldrik; Samson hasn't seen them for a time, and they can have a romp together.'

Her husband gazed at her fondly. 'Darling, we will all do exactly as you ask, but if I find you haven't curled up for at least two hours I shall beat you when I get home.'

They all laughed and then Aldrik said, 'Get your coat, Cressida, and we'll be off.' He gave Charity a quick kiss. 'Thanks for the lunch, my dear,' and he bent to kiss the little girls' cheeks. Whatever it was he said to them sent them running into the hall to search the pockets of his heavy jacket and find the chocolates he had brought with him. Cressida, tying a scarf over her tidy head, thought how happy everyone was. I'm happy too, she reflected, I suppose it's because I'm settled and everyone is so nice.

Sitting beside the doctor presently, driving along a narrow brick road between polder land, she said, 'Charity told me that you're going to England for Christmas. Do you go every year?'

He slid the car into an even narrower road. 'Usually; my grandmother is too old to travel over here. My mother spends Christmas with her but she is visiting one of my sisters. I don't like to think of the old lady being on her own.'

'You come back for New Year?'

'Oh, yes.'

'Then I expect you'll be getting married?'

He said drily, 'The idea had occurred to me. Should I be flattered at your interest, Cressida?'

She looked away from him out of the car window. 'Have I been nosy? I'm sorry. I—I was just making conversation.'

'Surely there is no need for us to have to do that? Let's talk instead.' He turned and smiled at her. 'I wonder if you will like my home—we're almost there, another mile or so. We're quite close to the sea now. As we go back we'll take the other road through Dokkum. Are you to be free on every Thursday?'

'I think so, and once a month I'm...' She stopped just in time from telling him that she would have a weekend to herself.

'Once a month?' he prompted.

'Oh, nothing,' she mumbled, 'nothing important.' She had gone pink; the very idea of telling him about her weekend... he might have thought that she was fishing for an invitation to go out with him. He was nice enough to have responded too even if he hadn't wanted to. She remembered how he had put himself out on her behalf and said hastily, 'Charity and I are going shopping together. It's lovely having her so close, I've—I've planned to do such a lot.'

He didn't reply and she was searching her head for a suitable topic of conversation when the road widened into a very small village square encircled by cottages, an austere church, two shops and a village school.

'Janslum,' said the doctor. 'I'm just up the lane.'

Cressida, with the vague idea of a smallish country house with a nice garden, was taken aback as he swept the car through an open gateway between high pillars and along a straight drive between small wintry blown trees. It curved presently and the house came into view.

'You live here?' gasped Cressida. 'All by yourself?'

'Not quite by myself,' he conceded, 'and later of course...'

'When you are married.' He had got out to open her door and help her and she stood beside him, looking at the house, white-walled and gabled with tall windows on either side of the porch, the windows above getting smaller and smaller until they reached the roof. There were lights shining from the downstairs rooms and as she looked the door was opened and she could see the hall beyond, aglow with soft lamp-light.

'It's perfect,' she said to no one in particular. 'Just right.'

CHAPTER SEVEN

THE doctor didn't say anything, but he smiled a little as he swept her indoors. 'This is Wester, who looks after the house for me. His wife Tyske does the cooking. I should sink without trace without them.'

West smiled discreetly and shook the hand Cressida held out.

'I've brought Miss Preece for tea,' explained the doctor. He glanced at his watch. 'There's plenty of time; would you like to look round the grounds, Cressida?'

'Oh, yes, please.'

'It's very nearly dark but there is a moon. Come this way...'

He led her round to the side of the house, down a few shallow steps and through a shrubbery. There was a gate at the end and as they reached it he asked, 'Do you like horses?'

'Horses? Me? Yes, I do. When Father was alive I used to ride with him. My stepmother sold Father's horse and my pony.' She bent down to fondle Caesar's ears and pat Mabel, pacing along beside her. The memory still hurt.

'Take a look at these,' invited the doctor cheerfully, and whistled. The two enormous beasts who loomed up at a gallop by the gate were followed by an old pony and a donkey.

'Heavens above—the size of them! They're percherons, aren't they? Do you work them?'

'Just when we make hay and plough. They're elderly—
I got them from the knackers—there's room enough for
them here and they deserve a year or two of peace and
quiet.'

She stroked the enormous noses breathing gently over
them. 'And the pony and donkey?'

'They happened to be there. The pony's very old, and
he and the donkey are fast friends.' He nodded towards
the end of the field beyond the gate. 'The stables are
over there. I've a mare I ride when I'm here—she's
already in for the night. The boy will be along soon to
bed these four down.'

He handed out lumps of sugar and Cressida said, 'Oh,
may I...?'

He gave her the rest of the sugar and she took off her
glove and offered it in turn. 'Oh, how can you bear not
to live here?' she wanted to know.

'Well, I have my work.' He smiled down at her.
'Holland is a small country and I have my car. I spend
as much time here as I can manage.' He broke off as a
strong-looking lad came plodding towards them. 'There's
Wigbald.' He called out to the boy who as he joined
them said something in Fries and the doctor replied in
the same tongue before saying, 'Cressida, this is Wigbald
who runs the stables for me and does the ploughing and
a good deal of the heavy work. He will be a good farmer
when he is grown.'

He spoke to Wigbald again, the boy came forward
and she held out a hand and had it wrung remorselessly.
'Nice to meet you,' said Cressida and smiled widely at
him, hoping he would at least see that she was pleased
to meet him. It seemed he was for he made quite a long
speech, not a word of which could she understand. He
then thumped the beasts gently on their enormous rumps

and turned to the stables, followed by the pony and the donkey.

Cressida watched their stately plodding until they had reached the stables. 'That's a very funny name,' she said. 'Wigbald—how do you spell it?'

The doctor obliged. 'Fries names are a little out of the ordinary and we like to keep them in the family, as it were.' He took her arm. 'You'll get cold standing there—my fault. We can walk round the shrubbery and cross the lawn and go in through the kitchen.'

It was almost dark now but the sky was clear and full of stars and coming out of the shrubbery on to the grass she saw the house again, the back this time, with lighted windows casting brightness on to the velvety lawn. Without stopping to think she said, 'But Nicola must be mad to dislike this—it's the most wonderful house I've ever seen.' She stopped abruptly. 'I'm sorry, I had no business to say that. I—I expect den Haag is a very nice place; some people prefer the town, don't they? I mean, it's really a long way from anywhere here, isn't it?' She went on a little desperately, for he had remained silent, 'Although I suppose Leeuwarden isn't too far away.'

'Don't babble, Cressy, there is no need.' He sounded kind and a little amused. They had reached a stout door at the bottom of a pair of steps and he led her down and opened it on to a flagged passage with plastered walls at the end of which there was another door. The kitchen was beyond, a large square room, its flagstones covered in matting, a row of windows at semi-basement level. A vast dresser loaded with china took up almost all of one wall and facing the door was a large Aga before which sat a tabby cat who ignored the dogs. Tyske was at the table, stuffing a chicken; she looked up as they went in and said something to the doctor which made him laugh.

'Tyske says that we must be cold and she will bring tea at once.'

What was there to laugh about in that? reflected Cressida as she was led out of the kitchen, up a few steps and through a small door which took them into the hall. The door was beside a wide staircase which ascended to a half-landing before turning at right angles to a gallery above. The house door was ahead of them and a wide sweep of black and white tiles, partly covered by thin silk rugs. Along one wall was a walnut side-table with a panelled frieze elaborately carved, upon which was a bowl of chrysanthemums, and on either side of it Dutch burgomaster chairs each with an intricately carved crest. On the opposite wall there was a marble fireplace in which a log fire burned briskly, flanked by winged armchairs, their walnut cabriole legs gleaming in the firelight, upholstered in dark red brocade. The walls were white and almost covered by portraits and landscapes in heavy gilt frames. A brass chandelier hung from the high plastered ceiling and there were ormolu wall lights spaced around the walls. A long case clock stood in one corner, chiming the hour.

She stood still, taking it all in unhurriedly. 'It's beautiful,' she said presently, and the doctor nodded.

'Most of the furniture is original and was brought here when the house was built.'

'It's old, the house...'

'Parts of it are sixteenth-century; it got added to from time to time but except for the plumbing and heating and electricity it hasn't been altered for almost two hundred years.'

They crossed to arched double doors and he ushered her through them into the drawing-room. There was a bright fire here too, under a massive stone hood with a coat of arms carved upon it. It was a very large room and yet it contrived to be lived-in and comfortable. The furniture was a nice mixture of satinwood and rosewood although the two walnut and marquetry display cabinets on either side of the fireplace were of an earlier date and filled with massive silver and a Meissen tea set, a collection of small bowls and dishes and a massive centrepiece.

There were sofas on either side of the fire and a number of easy-chairs and the room was lighted by the lamps standing on the various small tables. The enormous cut-glass chandelier hanging from the ceiling, although unlighted, reflected the lamp-light and the flames from the fire, giving the room a warm glow.

The doctor gave her time to look around before inviting her to sit by the fire. 'We'll have our tea here,' he said, sitting down opposite her, 'then we must go back; it wouldn't do to keep Charity waiting.'

Cressida said, 'You have a beautiful home and so peaceful and far away—well, I know you can't be far away from anywhere in Holland but it seems like that.'

'You like the country?'

'Oh, yes, although I liked Leiden. I'm going to explore this part of Holland...'

'Friesland.' He was laughing.

'Yes, well, Friesland.' She smiled at him a little shyly as the door opened and Wester came in with the tea-tray. The dogs, who had stayed in the kitchen to have their meal, came in with him, followed by the cat. The three of them sat down before the fire, the cat in the middle.

'What is his name?' asked Cressida.

'Smith! He adopted us a year or so ago; the dogs are devoted to him.'

Wester had set out the tea things, a plate of sand-
wiches, another of little cakes and *speculaas* on a table
between them and gone again.

'Be mother,' said the doctor. 'I have two lumps of
sugar.'

He was friendly in a casual fashion and she felt at ease
with him. She had been rather taken aback with the
grandeur of his home but he was so very much at ease
himself that she forgot to be shy. Besides, the conversation he carried on was calculated to set her mind at
rest: gardens and gardening, music and books,
Friesland's past history... They ate their tea in complete
harmony. Cressida had quite forgotten Nicola, and, as
for the doctor, although he hadn't forgotten her, he had
certainly dismissed her from his mind as a problem to
be dealt with at some not too distant date.

Cressida was disappointed that she hadn't seen more
of the house, but Aldrik hadn't suggested it and she
hadn't liked to ask; besides it was time for them to return.
She asked if she might go to the kitchen and say goodbye
to Tyske, 'For she gave us such a lovely tea,' she pointed
out, and then shook hands with Wester, who bowed over
her hand—just as though I were someone important,
she thought, not noticing the doctor's smile. Nicola,
when she had been to Janslum, had ignored Wester and
eaten the delicious lunch Tyske had prepared for them
without comment.

They didn't talk much as they drove back to the van
der Bronses' house, Cressida sat quietly, feeling the
warmth of the breath of the dogs on the back of her
neck whenever they leaned forward. She was happy; she
was having a lovely day off and she was going back to
a job that she was enjoying. She'd had no idea that half

a dozen children could be such fun even if they were hard work and took up every moment of her day.

At the house, as the doctor helped her out she did her best to thank him. 'I can't remember when I've had such a splendid time,' she told him. 'Thank you very much. There must have been so many other things you would have liked to have done—I'm sure you don't get much free time.'

She was thinking of Nicola now and wondered if she had minded the doctor spending a whole day away from her.

'It is I who thank you,' he told her. 'I'm always happy to come to my home here and it is an added pleasure to show it to someone. I'm glad you liked to see it.'

'Oh, I did like it, the horses and that lovely kitchen and the dogs.' She stopped, aware that she was probably boring him. 'Anyway,' she went on briskly, 'thank you.'

They were standing on the sweep before the door and although it was really very cold she felt nothing but a warm glow. She lifted a happy face to his and he bent and kissed her.

Charity, who had gone to the window and seen the car's headlights sweep up to the door said, 'Tyco, he's kissing her...'

Her husband lowered his newspaper. 'A quite normal thing to do, my love.'

'Yes—no, it isn't. He's supposed to be going to marry that Nicola...'

'I hardly think that Aldrik is likely to be firmly influenced by what he is supposed to be doing. I have known him for years—he does what he wants to do.'

Charity came away from the window. 'Oh, do you suppose...?'

Tyco abandoned his reading. 'My darling, let us suppose nothing but wait and see.'

'Men,' said Charity. 'You're so different from us.'

'What a good thing that is, my love.' He pulled her towards him and kissed her soundly.

Dinner was a pleasant meal. Teile and Letizia had been allowed to stay up and the talk was a mixture of childish chatter and light-hearted talk. No one mentioned Nicola, nor did they comment on Cressida's unfortunate stay at Noordwijk-aan-Zee, and when they had had their coffee and she reminded Charity that she would have to go back to the ter Beemstras' the doctor got up as well.

'I'll drop you off,' he observed, 'it's on my way.' Which it wasn't, but Cressida, still a little muddled as to the geography of her surroundings, didn't know that. She made her farewells, promising to go shopping with Charity on the following week, and got into the Bentley again. Aldrik hadn't spoken and the drive to the ter Beemstras' was short. She wished very much that he would kiss her again but he didn't, only went into the house with her, exchanged a few courteous remarks with the ter Beemstras, shook her hand and went away again, without expressing a wish to see her again.

'Oh, well,' reflected Cressida, getting ready for bed, 'why should he? I dare say it was his good deed for the day.'

However there had been no need to kiss her, and certainly not with such—she sought for a word—satisfaction. She had enjoyed it, although she reminded herself prudently that she had been kissed so seldom that it had stirred her rather more than it might have stirred any other girl—Nicola, for instance. Horrible girl, thought Cressida, as she closed her eyes, and I wonder what he's doing? Ringing her up, most likely, telling her what a boring afternoon he had. She drifted off to sleep.

The doctor was in his study with Mabel and Caesar, making notes for the lecture he was to give in Leiden in a few days' time. Telephoning Nicola hadn't entered his head and when he was interrupted by a phone call from her he frowned impatiently.

'Darling,' trilled Nicola, 'are you very lonely up there? Are you coming back tomorrow? There's the van Douws' dinner party—you haven't forgotten? I'm just off to have dinner with one or two friends, I'm so lonely without you.' And when he didn't answer, 'Aldrik?'

'Enjoy yourself,' he told her. 'I'll pick you up tomorrow evening about seven o'clock. I'm not lonely, I'm getting a good deal of work done.'

'Oh, work,' said Nicola. 'What have you done all day?'

He told her briefly.

'I'm so glad the poor girl has settled down at last,' said Nicola softly. 'I feel very badly about her unhappy stay at Tante Clotilde's. It was all my fault. I thought she was a working-class girl, used to household chores. I'm so relieved that she has a more suitable job now. I dare say she'll meet someone of her own sort—a farmer or a bank clerk—someone like that.'

The doctor thought of several replies but he uttered none of them. He said again, 'Enjoy your evening, Nicola. I'll see you tomorrow.'

He wrote without interruption for a time then he went into the drawing-room. The room looked beautiful in the light of the lamps and the fire welcomed him. He looked at the chair where Cressida had been sitting and wished that she was still there.

He went to sit by the fire, one arm round Mabel's vast shoulders, Caesar sprawled over his feet, and when Wester came in presently he told him to lock up and go to bed. The old house was quiet, he could hear the wind whistling in from the Waddenzee but it was a sound he loved. Cressida would like it too, he reflected; he would bring her here again and drive her to the flat coast to watch the wild sea breaking against the dykes. He thought that it would be some time before she trusted him completely and it would be necessary to disabuse her of the idea that he and Nicola were to marry. He had never mentioned marriage to Nicola although he had to admit that he had considered her for a wife. She was pretty, amusing, knew how to dress and would run his homes efficiently, although he was aware that no one who worked for him liked her, but he had known for some days now—weeks, he amended—that he wanted Cressida for his wife. What had begun as an act of kindness on his part had become the most important thing in life. He would need patience and time, but he was a patient man. That she liked him he was sure, but she was wary of him too, and not surprisingly after her miserable time with Jonkvrouw van Germert.

He would have to talk to Nicola. He had known that she wanted to marry him but he was certain that she had no love for him. She enjoyed his company—besides, he was a wealthy man and able to give her everything she wanted—but he was aware too that she could be just as fond of any man who could give her a secure future. She would have been a very suitable wife, of course, but he marvelled that he had ever considered her as his. With hindsight he saw now that she had been clever enough to adapt to his life and ideals so that he, wrapped up in his profession and heart-whole, had allowed the idea of

marrying her to enter his head. 'Something which must
be remedied,' he observed to the dogs, who cocked
friendly ears but made no move.

With Christmas barely two weeks away the ter Beemstra
household was a hive of activity. The house would be
full, Mevrouw ter Beemstra told Cressida: aunts and
uncles, grandparents, brothers and sisters would be
coming. 'There will be four more children.' She sounded
apologetic. 'Ten all told! You will manage? Baby's nurse
will help out, of course, and we will all assist you.'

Cressida assured her that she would manage in a voice
which disguised her uncertainty of this. True, it would
be for a few days only, and the children would probably
amuse themselves for a good deal of the time. She shut
her mind to the problem of getting ten children out of
bed and washed and dressed and returning the same
number to their beds each evening, but bridges should
never be crossed until one reached them.

The following week was largely taken up with the
making of paper chains, addressing of Christmas cards
and the secret tying up of presents, and her days were
filled. She was to go to Charity's again for her day off
and drive to Leeuwarden to shop, and if, at the back of
her mind, she had hoped to see Aldrik van der Linus or
even have news of him, she was to be disappointed.

Tyco came to fetch her after breakfast before going
to Leiden for the day, and at his house she got into the
Mini, settled Charity beside her and took them to
Leeuwarden at a careful pace, still not very happy about
driving on the other side of the road. Directed by Charity,
she parked the car at a hotel in the centre of the city
while Charity reserved a table for lunch before the pair
of them made for the shops.

It had been a splendid day, reflected Cressida in her bed that night; Charity was a dear and they had talked about everything under the sun—excepting Aldrik—and they had done their shopping to their entire satisfaction although Cressida's purse was woefully empty. Back at the house Tyco had been waiting for them, ready to entertain them with an account of his day at Leiden and then admire the presents Charity had bought. Teile and Letizia had come back then and everything had been bundled away out of sight before tea. Tyco had driven her back to the ter Beemstras' after dinner that evening and gone indoors with her to spend a few minutes with them, and when he left he told her in his kind voice that they looked forward to seeing her again as soon as Christmas was over. No one had mentioned Aldrik; she supposed that he was already in England.

There were flurries of snow from a leaden sky the next day and by the day before Christmas Eve the countryside looked like a Christmas card. The school holidays had started and Cressida spent a good deal of the time making snowmen in the grounds with the children, going for brisk walks whenever the snow stopped and overseeing the changing of shoes, the drying of parkas and the drinking of hot cocoa the moment they got indoors. It was an energetic life with no time to spare but she enjoyed it and the exercise and the children's cheerful company had put colour into her cheeks and a sparkle in her eyes. She had taught them a carol too—'Good King Wenceslas'—badgering them to get the words right while she thumped the piano in the playroom. Even little Lucia joined in and Cressida hoped that it would be proof of her efforts to teach the children English.

They had had a final rehearsal, Lucia had been whisked off to her bed by her nurse and Cressida was helping the children to tidy the room when the door opened and the doctor walked in.

His, 'Hello,' was addressed to everyone in the room. 'I was sent up on my own; everyone's bustling about downstairs.'

The children surged round him, for he had known the whole family for some years, all talking at once.

'English,' warned Cressida, raising her voice to be heard.

'Just for a minute we speak Fries, dear Cressy,' said Willum. 'It is Christmas.' He gave her a wide smile. 'And we have not seen Oom Aldrik for some time.'

'All right. Ten minutes, then. I'm going to see Nurse about something.'

She whisked herself out of the room without looking at the doctor. She had been so delighted to see him; she supposed it was the unexpectedness of his arrival which had made her feel so excited. She had imagined him to be in England by now—perhaps he wasn't going after all. Nicola, she felt sure, had very persuasive powers.

She found Anna, Baby's nurse, in the night nursery. Her small charge already asleep, she was tidying the chest of drawers, but she looked up as Cressida put her head round the door and gave a reluctant smile. They got on well now, but for the first few days Cressida had been hard put to it to convince the nurse that she had no intention of interfering with little Lucia's routine. For half an hour each day she came to the nursery and taught the moppet simple English but always with Anna there too.

Cressida marshalled her scanty knowledge of Dutch, seeking permission for Lucia to stay up a little later on Christmas Eve so that she might sing the carol with her brothers and sisters. It took a few minutes to make herself understood and another few minutes while they exchanged remarks about the weather, and, having shown willing, as it were, Cressida went back to the playroom.

The doctor was still there. 'Ah, good, Cressy, will you come downstairs with me? There's something I want to give you...'

'It may be for us; is it?' asked Friso.

'That's something you'll know on Christmas morning, and don't tease Cressy to find out what it is, for she won't tell.'

The little girls kissed him and the boys shook his hand and screamed, 'Happy Christmas!' as he opened the door and ushered Cressida through.

He made no effort to go downstairs but stood looking down at her.

'Do you not wish that you were coming with me to England?' he asked.

She didn't answer at once while she thought about it. 'Well, I'd love to go home, but only if my stepmother wasn't there, if you see what I mean, and I'd like to see Moggy, but I'm really happy here. I felt, well, a stranger in Leiden, but here I feel quite at home, which is funny because half the time I don't understand a word of what anyone says.'

He laughed, 'I'm not surprised, Fries is a strange language, and the Hollanders don't understand it either. Will you be free at Christmas?'

'Heavens, no. The house will be full of family and there are four more children coming.'

'I must make it up to you when I get back...'

'Thank you, you're very kind, but there's no need. I mean, you've done such a lot for me already and you don't have much time and when you do you must have friends—and things to do...'

'Am I being snubbed, Cressy?' he asked blandly.

''Snubbed?' She was so shocked at the idea that she put a hand on his arm. 'How could I ever snub you? I don't know what I should have done without you.'

She stared up into his face, suddenly and blindingly aware that she didn't know what she *would* do without him; moreover the prospect of it didn't bear thinking about. She said slowly, 'I think you don't need to be concerned about me any longer, I mean you can forget me without feeling you need to bother. I don't think I am explaining myself very well but you've your own life and it's quite different from mine... Oh, dear, I really can't explain...'

'Then don't try,' he advised her briskly. 'Enjoy life here and have a happy Christmas.' He patted her hand in a big-brotherly way and added, 'Come down to the hall and get the parcel I've got for the children. I still have to call on the van der Bronses and then go to Janslum before I drive down to the ferry.'

She longed to ask him if Nicola was going with him but all she said was, 'I hope you have a lovely Christmas and please remember me to Lady Merrill.'

She went downstairs and he gave her a brightly wrapped box. 'I'd be grateful if you'd hide it away for them.' She wished very much that he would kiss her but he didn't, he wished her goodbye and went in search of Beatrix ter Beemstra, and within a few minutes he had driven himself away.

Cressida went slowly back upstairs, hid the box under the bed in her room and went back to the children. They were all excited and noisy and she had her hands full for the next twenty minutes or so, calming them down and making sure that they were clean and neat for their supper, a meal everyone was to share for once seeing that the household was involved in getting ready for the guests who were coming in the morning. The meal over, she got them to their beds and then went to Mevrouw ter Beemstra's room to pin up a dress that she had discovered at the last minute was too long.

Mevrouw ter Beemstra stood patiently while Cressida pinned, a little puzzled because Cressida was so quiet and pale. 'You feel well?' she asked anxiously. 'You are to tell me if there is anything? You are not unhappy?'

Cressida assured her that she had never felt better and there was nothing the matter. She made her voice cheerful, adding, 'I'm looking forward to Christmas very much; it's such fun with children, isn't it?'

Mevrouw ter Beemstra had been pursuing her own train of thought. 'Of course, Aldrik came to see you and I think that you wish that you could have gone to England with him? Is that not so? Such a kind man, he brought the children a present—he never forgets.'

Cressida, her mouth full of pins, was unable to answer. He'd forgotten her, hadn't he? Telling her to enjoy life in that brisk manner. At the moment she felt as though she would never enjoy life again as long as she lived and if this was how one felt when one found oneself in love then the quicker one fell out of love again the better.

She sat back on her heels to see the effect of her work and began a bright conversation with her employer which put that kind lady's mind at rest, and then she took the dress along to Anna, who sewed beautifully and was waiting with a needle and thread. Since it was quite late by now Cressida took herself off to bed and had a nice comfortable cry before she went to sleep. She woke up quite early in the morning feeling sensible and clear-

headed about the whole thing. It was most unfortunate
that she should have fallen in love with the doctor but
that wouldn't and mustn't alter the mild friendship he
had shown towards her, and now that she had made it
clear that she was nicely settled in a job and perfectly
happy he could forget her, and, no doubt, in the course
of time, marry Nicola. It was a fate she didn't want for
him, but if he loved the woman there was nothing she
could do about it. If, on the other hand, he didn't love
her, then, Cressida decided, she would do her best to
stop him getting married. She had no idea how she was
going to do this but it was an uplifting thought and
carried her through an extremely busy morning. The four
children arrived before lunch and since there were now
so many they were to have their meal in the playroom
with Cressida presiding. Quite a tableful, she conceded,
handing out plates of soup and acting as mediator between the two older boys and their cousins. The little
girls were over-excited too and she was relieved when the
meal was finished and she could get them into hats and
coats and allow them to stream into the garden to fight
each other with snowballs, and, with her help, make a
series of snowmen.

It was too cold to stay out for long, so she shepherded
them indoors again, saw to their tea and then sent them
all to collect the presents they had parcelled up so la-
boriously. They were to be put under the Christmas tree
that evening and handed out in the morning and there
was a good deal of stealthy coming and going until all
the presents were arranged on a table in the hall ready
for Mijnheer ter Beemstra to put under the tree later that
evening. Since it was such a special day all the children
were to stay up for supper which meant scrambling into
best clothes, and, for the girls, having their hair ar-

ranged just so. Cressida barely had time to get into the grey jersey dress, of which she was heartily sick, and do her own face and hair before the gong sounded and she lined up the children and set them in a tidy queue to go down to the drawing-room, bringing up the rear with Anna and little Lucia.

The drawing-room was a large room very full of people. Cressida had been introduced to everyone who had arrived but now they all looked alike to her; moreover, the women were wearing smart, expensive dresses. She stuck out like a sore thumb, and she wished that she had a uniform like Anna. She was a sensible girl, though; she had no intention of spoiling her evening by moaning over her unsuitable clothes. She made the rounds with the children, shaking hands with everyone and exchanging small talk, and found herself presently with a glass in her hand, talking to a rather fierce old gentleman who reminded her that he was Mevrouw ter Beemstra's father. He spoke English but insisted that she tried out her few words of Dutch. 'If you are going to stay here,' he rumbled, 'you'll have to speak the language.' He studied her face. 'I hear the children are doing well. You like teaching?'

'Well, I don't teach much, you know, just speak English all the time and they learn bits of poetry and that sort of thing. They're nice children and very quick.'

They were joined by an elderly lady, one of the aunts, Cressida supposed, who asked her how she liked Friesland, and since her English was only a little better than Cressida's Dutch the old gentleman amused himself helping them out until the gong went again and they trooped into the dining-room.

It looked very festive with tinsel decorations and a lovely centrepiece of holly and Christmas roses, and as

well as the large dining table a smaller one had been set
at right angles to it and here the children sat with Cressida
at one end and Anna at the other.

The meal was a leisurely one, and, since the children
were there, not elaborate: soup, little pastry parcels which
were filled with smoked salmon, roast pheasant with
straw potatoes and braised celery and finally ices topped
with whipped cream and nuts. Lucia was half asleep by
the time they had finished but she woke at once when
Willum reminded her in a loud voice that they were going
to sing their carol. Carefully coached by Cressida, he
got to his feet and announced that if everyone would go
to the drawing-room they would be entertained with a
Christmas carol, whereupon everyone clapped and made
haste to do as he asked, followed, when everyone was
settled, by the children. There was a grand piano in the
drawing-room, Cressida sat down at it as the children
filed into their places and she began on the well-known
tune. The children sang beautifully. One of them, she
wasn't sure which one, was tone deaf, but it hardly
showed and they had learnt the words carefully. The ap-
plause was deafening and they sang it all over again
before doing the rounds once more, bidding everyone
goodnight. As they were going out of the room Mevrouw
ter Beemstra said, 'Do come down again if you like,
Cressida.' She glanced at the clock. 'It is already late
but if you wish...'

Cressida thanked her, but agreed that it was late, she
didn't add that there were ten children to see into their
beds, which, even with Anna's help, would take quite
some time. She wished the room in general goodnight
and went upstairs, where the more rebellious of the
children had to be rounded up, stood over while they
cleaned their teeth and then tucked up in bed.

She went to bed herself almost at once, too tired to do more than wonder if Aldrik had reached his grandmother's house safely. Also she wondered if and when she would see him again.

CHAPTER EIGHT

CRESSIDA was so tired at the end of Christmas Day that she could have fallen on to her bed and gone to sleep without even bothering to undress, but she resisted the urge to do this, undressed, had a bath and got into bed, where she lay sleepily reviewing her day. It had been an exceedingly busy one but she had enjoyed every minute of it. The children had been a handful, of course; keeping the peace between ten children all tearing open their presents at the same time when they should have been having their breakfast had been a Herculean task, but, as Mevrouw ter Beemstra had pointed out, they would never have sat through morning church otherwise and going to church in the village on Christmas morning was a tradition which had to be maintained. There had been no turkey or Christmas pudding at lunch, but vegetable soup followed by goose with red cabbage and then a spectacular dessert of ice-cream, whipped cream and fresh pineapple had proved excellent substitutes, and there had been champagne for the grown-ups and fruit drinks for the children. There was no question of a respite after the meal; the children had been buttoned into their outdoor clothes again and left loose in the garden with Cressida in charge. What afternoon there was left had been more than filled by the need to assist the smaller ones to learn to ride their tricycles and bicycles, set up a target so that the older boys could try out their air pistols and keep the peace between the little girls, casting eyes on each other's dolls and wanting them. They had

had tea in the playroom and then played grandmother's footsteps and hunt the slipper, games they had never heard of but which Cressida remembered very well from her own childhood and which tired them out nicely. They had had their supper in the small sitting-room leading from the drawing-room and the next hour or so was entirely taken up with marshalling them tidily so that they could say goodnight to the grown-ups in the drawing-room and then be coaxed to their beds after their baths. Cressida reflected that she could have gone to bed herself then quite happily but the ter Beemstras had insisted that she should join everyone else for a buffet supper, so she had changed into the grey jersey and gone back downstairs, where she had been instantly made at home by Mevrouw ter Beemstra, handed from countless cousins and aunts and uncles once again and thanked for the care she had had for the children.

She was plied with drink too and delicious bits and pieces, and presently found herself sitting by the *domine*, a youngish man with a rather stern face. His English was good and he was interested in her; she found herself talking freely to him although she said nothing about her unfortunate stay with Jonkvrouw van Germert, but she did talk about the doctor because he was always at the back of her mind and thinking about him wasn't enough. The *domine* listened gravely. 'You have been lucky to have found such a good and kind friend,' he had told her. 'You will be grateful to him for the rest of your life.'

'Yes, I expect I shall,' Cressida had said quietly. Her companion had made it seem as though the doctor had been an episode in her life to be remembered with gratitude but never to be revived.

She had wished everyone goodnight presently and gone up to her room and to her bed. It had really been a very happy day, she muttered sleepily; she had had presents too, handkerchiefs and notepaper and a charming silver bracelet. She should have been feeling happy. It was strange therefore that she should cry herself to sleep.

She woke during the night. 'He could have sent me a Christmas card,' she said sadly, and presently she went to sleep again.

She was up early and soon was urging the children out of their beds and into their clothes and all the while the doctor loomed at the back of her mind, and that despite the fact that she had wakened with the intention of thinking no more about him.

An intention not upheld by Aldrik van der Linus, however. He had thought of her constantly and in answer to his grandmother's discreet probings had made no bones about telling her that it was his intention to marry Cressida.

His grandmother received the news without surprise. 'A sweet girl,' she had told him, 'and very sensible too. Has she any idea...?'

'No. I had hoped that we would become friends and in a sense we are, but although she doesn't blame me for her unfortunate stay with Jonkvrouw van Germert she is under the impression that I intend to marry Nicola. I shall need to go carefully.'

'You have made things clear to Nicola?'

'Yes, if by that you mean that she doesn't expect to marry me; indeed she assured me that she had never considered me as a prospective husband and was only too delighted that I had fallen in love at last.'

To which his grandmother made no reply. Men, reflected that lady silently, could be so blind, and the cleverer they were the blinder they seemed to be. Nicola, she had no doubt, had every intention of marrying him; he was too good a prize to give up. She said merely, 'You must be relieved that Cressida is so happy.'

'Indeed I am. I shall go and see her as soon as possible after I get back to Janslum. I have some patients to see in Leiden and a short list at the hospital but I should be able to manage a day or two after that.'

Cressida, unaware of this, busied herself with the children, thankful when the four young visitors departed for their homes once more. Six, she reflected, were manageable, but ten were a bit too much.

The weather was still wintry with flurries of snow and biting winds, but the children seemed impervious to this; wrapped in her elderly winter coat and a pair of borrowed wellies, a woolly cap pulled down over her ears and a scarf tied round her neck, she accompanied them on expeditions to many nearby canals and a small lake, where they donned their skates and spent hours racing to and fro, and after the first day, realising that she would freeze to death if she didn't do something about it, she prevailed upon Willum to lend her a pair of old skates—Friesian skates, he told her in his careful English, just right for learners—and with his help and a good deal of encouragement from the other children she ventured upon the ice. Of course she fell over a great deal, to be hauled to her feet with commendable patience by Willum or Jacobus, but the by the end of the second day she was able to stagger a few steps on her own and even manage a short distance with the boys, once they were on either side of her, clasping her hands, before she lost her nerve and fell, spiralling slowly on to the ice.

By the end of the week though she was striking out boldly on her own, still falling a good deal of course, amid peals of laughter from the children, but smugly pleased with herself.

She told Charity about it when she went to spend her free day with her. 'I'm black and blue,' she confided, 'but it's such fun and it keeps the children amused.'

'You're still happy? The ter Beemstras are kind to you?'

'Oh, yes, and once the children go back to school I shall have more time... Everyone seems to be getting excited about New Year...'

'Oh, yes, *Olie Ballen* and champagne. Great fun. Are the ter Beemstras having a house party? We've got Tyco's family coming again. Usually we go there but he doesn't want me to go too far from home...'

Cressida nodded. 'Quite right too. Yes, there is to be a houseful again. Willum is to be allowed to stay up this year; Jacobus and Friso are furious about it. The other four children won't be coming though so once I get them to bed the others should be manageable.' She smiled widely. 'They are sweet, you know, even when they're naughty.'

Charity looked at her anxiously. 'You don't regret being there? You might have got a much cushier job in England.'

'What as? I can't do anything, you know—only housework and the flowers and fetching and carrying. Children are much more fun. Besides, they keep me very busy.'

The next day the guests arrived; aunts and uncles, cousins, old friends—Cressida had met most of them at

Christmas. They greeted her kindly, observed in their excellent English how well she coped with the children, and looked forward to seeing her that evening at dinner.

Cressida, getting into the grey dress—which she never wished to see again—reflected that so far everything was going well. The children had gone to bed like lambs and she actually had time on her hands before going down to the drawing-room. She went along to the playroom and sat down in a window-seat, looking out into the dark night. It had stopped snowing and presently there would be a moon but now there was the merest glimmer of stars. She stared up at them and wondered where the doctor was. Back in his lovely home, no doubt, with Nicola and a houseful of guests.

His, 'Hello, Cressy', was so part and parcel of her thoughts that she took a moment to realise that he was actually there, in the room, leaning against the door, still in his heavy car coat, bringing a blast of icy air from the cold night into the room.

'Well,' said Cressida, 'well, what a surprise.' She was aware that this didn't sound very welcoming or friendly and added hastily, 'I mean, how nice to see you, Doctor.'

He came to stand before her, looming over her, blotting out the room with his vast size, and since he said nothing she plunged into speech.

'You're not staying here of course—you're on your way to Janslum. I expect you have a houseful of guests; I had no idea that New Year was so important in Holland...'

'Friesland,' he corrected her smilingly. 'Oh, but it it. We come miles in order to celebrate it and wish each other well. My sisters and their husbands and children will be at home waiting for me...'

'And Mabel and Caesar and the horses, pony and donkey,' said Cressida in a far-away voice, 'and that nice Wester and his wife.' She sat up—this would never do; on no account must he feel sorry for her. She went on briskly, 'I expect you had a happy Christmas? I hope Lady Merrill is well?'

'In excellent health. She sends you her love. Are you happy, Cressida?'

She hadn't expected that so that she answered too quickly. 'Oh, yes. The children are such fun and Mevrouw and Mijnheer ter Beemstra are so kind. We had a lovely time at Christmas.' She went pink, for it had sounded as though she was reminding him that he had ignored her completely, although he had no reason to have done otherwise. She hurried on, anxious to let him see just how happy she was. 'The children have taught me to skate, I'm not good at it yet, but I can stay on my feet for a little while. It's been very cold here and there's been a lot of snow.'

She looked up and caught his eyes. There was a gleam in them which she thought was amusement and indeed she was making a fine hash of a casual conversation.

He bent down and drew her to her feet and laid his hands on her shoulders. 'I came to wish you a happy New Year, Cressy,' he told her, 'and it will be, you know.' He kissed her gently on her cheek, looking down at her gravely. 'I thought of you while I was in England.'

She was suddenly very cross. 'Oh, did you?' she asked, peeved. 'Then why didn't you send me a Christmas card? Lady Merrill sent me one and so did Moggy and her sister and Mr Tims.' She drew in her breath like a child. 'I'm sorry, I didn't mean any of that, truly I didn't. You've been so kind to me and I shall always be grateful. Perhaps I'm tired.' She smiled shakily. 'I hope you have a marvellous New Year with lots of patients and everything you could possibly wish for.'

'Well, not too many patients,' he was laughing a little, 'and I intend to have everything I wish for. Do you know what I wish for, Cressy?'

The door opened and Willum came in and the doctor took his hands from Cressida's shoulders and said easily, 'Hello, Willum, do you want Cressy?'

'Yes, I can't find the tie I had for Christmas—the green one—I want to wear it.' He added importantly, 'I'm staying up for dinner.'

'Splendid.' The doctor didn't sound in the least put out at the interruption. It couldn't have been anything important, thought Cressida; perhaps he had been going to tell her that he was going to marry Nicola, and that they had made up their differences. She was a clever enough young woman to convince him that she had been acting for the best when she had arranged for Cressida to go to her aunt and he would have forgiven her.

The doctor said softly, 'No, Cressida, don't try and guess. Wait until I tell you.' He went to the door. 'I must be off or it will be after midnight before I get home and that wouldn't do at all. I'll wish you both a happy New Year and leave you to find that tie.'

He went away and Cressida heard a good deal of laughter in the hall downstairs and then the solid sound of the front door shutting.

'Let's go and look for it,' she told Willum.

Dinner was elaborate and festive and afterwards everyone went to the drawing-room and drank champagne and ate the *Olie Ballen*. They were nice, Cressida decided, like small doughnuts, each encased in a paper napkin to keep the grease and sugar off the guests' clothes, and presently their glasses were filled once again and as the great *stoelklok* in the corner of the room chimed midnight, a toast was drunk to the New Year and everyone went around kissing each other and shaking hands. Someone turned on the record player and several people started to dance, the signal for Cressida to capture a reluctant Willum, bid everyone goodnight and see him safely into his bed. She didn't go downstairs again; it had been a lovely evening and the very best bit of it had been Aldrik's visit. Although, she thought sleepily, it had been a pity that Willum had had to come into the room when he had. Of course she knew that sooner or later the doctor would marry Nicola, she was so exactly right for a well-known doctor, but it would have clinched the matter, so to speak, if he had told her himself; she was finding it hard to plan her future but she thought in a muddled way that it might be easier once he was married.

After the excitement of the New Year the days were rather dull but very soon the boys went back to school so that the pattern of her days was changed again. She was still fully occupied but now she had an hour or two free during the day, which she occupied by exploring the village and the surrounding countryside. It was on the second day that she went for an expedition that she met the *domine* again and was invited to look round the church with him. She liked him and she was eager to learn all that she could about Friesland and the people who lived there, and he for his part seemed pleased to tell her all that he knew. The church disappointed her; it was white-washed and rather bare although the pulpit with its sounding-board was very handsome, but it had a long and interesting history and she was a willing listener. Before she left him he invited her to go again so that she might look at the church registers. She accepted willingly; it was nice to have a friend and very soon now Charity would have her baby and there would be an end to their shopping expeditions at least for the time being. She told Mevrouw ter Beemstra about it when she got back and that lady nodded approvingly; Domine Stilstra was a serious man, no longer young but well liked by everybody. It crossed her mind that it wouldn't be a bad thing if he were to marry; Cressida would make him a most suitable wife... She observed kindly, 'Domine Stilstra is a most interesting man; he knows so much of our history and spends a great deal of his time studying old customs.'

It had stayed cold and the canals and ponds were frozen solid although the sun had shone from time to time, but two days after Cressida's tour of the church the sky became overcast and the wind, always cold, became bitter. None the less Anna wrapped herself and Lucia warmly and declared her intention of going to see her sister who lived on the other side of the village. Mevrouw ter Beemstra had gone to Leeuwarden to the hairdressers and Cressida, struggling for the right words to persuade her not to go, found her vocabulary quite inadequate. To her anxious arm waving in the direction of the darkening cloudy sky, Anna merely smiled and patted her shoulder with a reassuring, 'OK.'

Cressida dredged up what she hoped were the right words and asked if Anna would be back for playroom tea, whereupon Anna broke into a long reply, which, since she couldn't make head or tail of it, did little to reassure Cressida. She watched the two of them go with the unhappy feeling that she should have stopped them; on the other hand probably she was being fussy. After all, Anna had lived in Friesland all her life and would know the weather like the back of her hand.

She didn't go out herself. Both Sepke and Galske were at home, sharing, as they shared everything, a nasty cold. She settled them by the playroom stove, with a packet of tissues and their favourite toys, and then got out the mending basket and began on the task of repairing a rent in one of Friso's shirts. The afternoon darkened rapidly and she drew the curtains and turned on the lights, listening worriedly to the wind howling across the empty fields. Presently she went downstairs to see if Anna and Lucia were back but there was no sign of them and although she was partly reassured by the cook's unworried face she wished that Mevrouw ter Beemstra were at home.

They had their tea and there was still no sign of any one of them and when she heard the car stopping outside the house she ran downstairs intent on telling Mijnheer ter Beemstra. As she reached the front door she saw its tail lights disappearing again and Willum told her that his father had to return at once to his office. 'What do you want him for?' he asked.

'Oh, well, I dare say it's all right but Anna and Lucia are still out—I expected them back for tea. Your mother will be back presently and she'll know what to do. Come along upstairs, you're all three cold and wet...is the weather very bad outside?'

'Very bad, and there is warning of a storm,' said Willum. 'I hope that our mother takes care.'

'She's a very good driver,' said Cressida cheerfully, and tried to ignore a particularly violent gust of wind howling round the house.

She had the boys settled at the table eating their tea when Mevrouw ter Beemstra returned. She heard her voice in the hall and went down to meet her.

'The weather is very bad,' said Mevrouw ter Beemstra. 'It is difficult to drive. The children are safe home?'

'Anna and Lucia went out after lunch and they are not back. I came down to tell *Mijnheer* when he brought the boys back but he didn't stop only drove away at once. Anna said she was going to her sister's; perhaps she is still there?'

Mevrouw ter Beemstra looked worried. 'She would never stay if she saw that the weather was worsening. I am so afraid that she has taken the short-cut across the fields—it is only a short distance that way and she may have thought she could get back here before the storm broke... We have had a warning of severe wind, I must go and see...'

'I'll go,' said Cressida. 'It's the path leading from the end of the garden at the back of the house, isn't it? Willum pointed out the cottage to me one day, I'm sure that I can find it. If I have a torch it won't be difficult.'

Brave words. She was scared of going out into the dark evening but perhaps Anna and Lucia were sheltering somewhere along the path, not too far away, afraid to go on without a light.

'I'll get my boots—if I could have a powerful torch.'

She was ready to go within five minutes, seen out of the kitchen door by Mevrouw ter Beemstra. 'Don't worry if we don't get back quickly; if Anna is near enough to her sister's cottage, I'll take them back there until the worst of the storm is over. Can it be reached from the village?'

'By car, no. At least a Range Rover could get to within a short distance but there's a canal...'

Mevrouw ter Beemstra looked as though she was going to cry and Cressida said quickly, 'Don't worry, they can't be far away. They may still be with Anna's sister. If they are, I'll come back and tell you.'

She turned on the torch, reassured by its powerful beam, and started with haste down the path which led to the end of the grounds at the back of the house.

The wind was terrific, tearing at her clothes and the scarf she had tied round her head. The rain was ice-cold and the ground beneath her feet treacherous with ice too. She shone the torch before her until she reached the path and then went even more slowly, for she was walking into the teeth of the wind now and could hardly keep on her feet. Every few yards she stopped and shone the torch round her in the hope that she might see Anna and Lucia. It seemed unlikely, there was no shelter and no hedges, only frozen canals between the fields, narrow enough to jump over. There was a much wider canal further on, she knew, with a rickety bridge over it. The thought of having to cross it made her feel sick but the cottage was only a few hundred yards from it and there was no other way. Reaching it, she eyed it fearfully and actually had one hand on the flimsy wooden rail when she heard a sound, and when the wind paused in its bellowing she heard it again. She turned the torch in all directions, lighting up the fields around her and then shone it on to the canal. Anna was crouched on the bank, shielding Lucia with her body.

Cressida gave a wobbly shout and started towards her at the same time as the rain turned to blinding snow. It blotted out everything, whirling round her, driven by the wind and for a moment she stood still, making quite sure that she hadn't moved since she spotted Anna, then she moved carefully forward, praying that she wasn't going round in a circle, and to her relief saw them only a yard or two away.

Crouched down beside them, she could see that Anna's face was very white. Her Dutch deserted her, all she could think of to say was, 'OK?' At least it was a start. Anna shook her head and pointed to one leg.

'*Gebroken*', she muttered, and then urgently, 'Lucia?'

The child was almost asleep with the cold and the pulse in the small wrist was faint, as far as Cressida could tell, though, she wasn't hurt. It was poor Anna who needed urgent help; she must be in pain, thought Cressida and she was lying awkwardly, shielding the little girl's body with her own.

'I'm going to get help,' said Cressida, and added, '*hulp*' and held up five fingers, hoping that Anna would understand that she would be gone for five minutes. That was nonsense, of course, she would never get back in five minutes, but it helped to look on the bright side.

She got to her feet, numb with the cold, patted Anna on the shoulder and started back the way she had come. Hopefully anyone watching from the house would see her torch and come to meet her. She didn't know how long Anna and Lucia had been lying there but Lucia had seemed half asleep despite her whimpers and Anna must surely be half frozen to death. The thought sent her scurrying along the slippery path and she fell down almost at once. The ground was iron-hard and she had to scramble painfully to her feet as best she could before going on more cautiously.

'More haste, less speed,' said Cressida, in a rage with herself, the wind and snow and the terrifying feeling that she was alone in a strange world. She had dropped the torch too, but luckily it was not broken. She picked it up and shone it ahead of her and was almost blinded by the beam from another torch. It was too much; she screamed and was instantly engulfed in the doctor's great arms.

'Silly girl, it is I!' he bellowed into her ear.

Even in a trying situation such as this, she thought, he gets his grammar right, and she promptly burst into tears.

'Where are they?' he asked her, shouting into the wind.

She waved behind her. 'Anna's hurt her leg—I was coming to get help. I think Lucia is all right.'

'Stop crying.' He spoke close to her ear. 'Just where?'

Unfeeling brute, she reflected and then pulled herself together. 'By the canal on the left...'

'Stay here, on no account move.' He kissed her quite roughly and was gone, leaving her almost frozen solid but with a warm glow under her ribs on account of the kiss.

He was a great deal quicker than she had been—in no time at all he was back with Lucia in his arms. He dumped the child on to Cressida, stayed only long enough to warn her to stay where she was and disappeared into the snowy darkness once again.

He was a little longer this time. Not surprisingly, for Anna was a well-built woman and unconscious now—a dead weight.

'Follow me and don't lag behind,' he ordered Cressida, something she had no intention of doing anyway, and she stumbled along as close as she could manage with Lucia hugged close to her, crying now and wanting her mama.

It seemed a long time before they reached the end of the path and saw the lights of the house shining and then a sudden surge of people coming towards them through the snow. Someone—she thought it was Mijnheer ter Beemstra—took Lucia from her, and she straightened her cramped arms and plodded on. She was very tired now and the doctor was somewhere ahead of her, lost in the whirling snowflakes. The house was quite close now, she heaved a sigh of relief and tripped over her own numb feet and once more fell down.

It was really too much trouble to get up. She stayed where she was, aware that it was a foolish thing to do, but she couldn't be bothered to make the effort. She was so cold that it didn't matter any more. She closed her eyes—a nap would be pleasant.

In the house there was ordered chaos with the doctor issuing instructions with unhurried calm. Lucia to her mother, to be undressed and put into a warm—not hot—bath and then into bed, given hot milk and not left until he had had time to look at her. Anna was laid on the kitchen table, divested of as much clothing as possible, wrapped in blankets and then examined.

Her leg was broken, he knew that already—a Pott's fracture just above the ankle. She was still unconscious and he was able to pull the bones into alignment with the help of Mijnheer ter Beemstra, who had just arrived, apply temporary splints and bandage the limb. He had just finished this when he said, 'Where is Cressida? I'd better take a look at her—she'll need bed and warmth...'

She wasn't to be found. Leaving a slowly recovering Anna to the care of the cook, Aldrik got into his coat again, his face grim, and, armed with a torch once more, went back out into the night. He found her quite quickly, for she had been within shouting distance when she fell. He dropped on a knee beside her and shone the torch in her face and let out a great gusty sigh. She was already asleep, she was also ice-cold and her pulse was slow and faint. He lifted her carefully and carried her back to the

house and into the warm kitchen, where he found Cook
and Mijnheer ter Beemstra hovering over Anna.

'Dirk, get on to the hospital in Leeuwarden, will you?
As soon as possible Lucia and Anna must get there for
a check-up and so must Cressida.'

He put her down comfortably into Cook's large chair
and took off the wellies and her gloves and then, helped
by the housemaid, her coat and sodden headscarf. 'Fetch
some blankets, will you?' he asked the girl, and went to
look at Anna, conscious once more, and then upstairs
to see Lucia, who was already, with the resilience of the
young, almost her small self again.

Back in the kitchen he found Cressida rousing.

'However did you get here?' she wanted to know, and
then peevishly, 'You should know better than to travel
in this weather.'

He was taking her pulse, now satisfactorily normal.
'I was on my way to Janslum—I called to see how you
were getting on.'

He took the warm milk Cook had fetched and held
it for her while she sipped. 'You will go to Leeuwarden
for a check-up,' he told her with impersonal kindness.
'I think you are perfectly all right but all the same you
must be examined. Lucia and Anna will go too.'

'Now?'

'Yes, in my car. Anna and Lucia will go with Dirk ter
Beemstra, but we shall have to wait until the blizzard
has blown out.'

He made her drink the rest of the milk and spoke to
the housemaid.

'You will go upstairs and get into a warm bath and
put on dry clothing; Sierou will go with you.' He nodded
to the maid and Cressida got to her feet. She peered out
at him from her cocoon of blankets.

'Why did you kiss me like that?' she wanted to know.

He showed no surprise at her question. 'Shall we say that it was a happy meeting?' He smiled a little. 'Run along now and do as I say.'

Half an hour later she was downstairs again wearing one of Mevrouw ter Beemstra's winter coats. It had a hood and was a great deal too large but it was beautifully warm. That lady had wept over her when she had gone to see how Lucia was. 'I'll never be able to thank you enough, Cressida. You have been so brave.' She shuddered. 'And if Aldrik hadn't come along when he did, what would have happened?'

'Well, he did come,' said Cressida bracingly, 'and everything is all right. Poor Anna—she was so brave, crouching over Baby although her leg must have hurt dreadfully.'

They went downstairs together and found Aldrik and Dirk ter Beemstra carrying Anna to Dirk's car. The children, forbidden to come downstairs from the playroom until everything was normal again, had taken up position on the landing and were watching through the banisters.

'Come back, Cressida,' Willum called, 'we shall miss you.'

Cressida waved to them. '*Tot ziens*,' she replied, airing her Dutch.

Leeuwarden wasn't far away but the journey, even undertaken by the two men who knew the road like the backs of their hands and were skilled drivers, took on the aspect of a nightmare. Cressida, bundled in rugs beside Aldrik with the dogs' warm breath on her neck, cowered in her seat each time the car skidded. The snow had eased a little and so had the wind but it wasn't the night for a drive.

The doctor drove steadily and apparently without any
fears for their safety and while he drove he kept up a
steady flow of small talk so that she was forced to answer
him and take her mind off the possibility of them
skidding into a canal or going full tilt into a snowdrift;
all the same she couldn't help asking just once if they
were nearly there.

'Yes. Don't be frightened, Cressy, I won't let anything
harm you.'

He was reassuringly calm and she felt ashamed of her
fears and mumbled, 'Oh, I know, I know. I'm quite
sure—I don't feel quite me or I wouldn't be such a
coward.'

'Cressy, cowards don't walk out into a blizzard with
only a torch and a guardian angel.' He actually laughed
then, righted the Bentley out of a skid and drove on.

He got them to the hospital and they kept her in that
night. They kept Lucia in too, and Anna was to stay for
a day or two while her leg was put in plaster and she
learned how to manage the crutches. That she hadn't
got pneumonia was a miracle. Cressida, who had been
whisked away to be examined and put to bed, had no
chance to do more than bid Aldrik a hasty goodbye; she
could only hope that he reached his home fairly safely
through the appalling weather.

Dirk ter Beemstra came the next day and fetched her
and Lucia home; the blizzard had blown itself out, the
sun shone and the snow ploughs had cleared the main
roads. Everything was back to normal in a surprisingly
short time—excepting for Cressida's heart, which she was
sure would never be normal again. Beyond Dirk ter
Beemstra's casual remark that Aldrik had got home
safely she heard nothing of the doctor and she had been
too shy to ask for news of him. Besides, the household

was entirely disrupted for several days; she had stepped into Anna's shoes temporarily and she had more than enough to do to fill her days and thoughts.

A week went by, Anna came back and spurned the cosseting Mevrouw ter Beemstra would have given her. She stumped around on her crutches, only relinquishing Lucia to Cressida's care for her daily walk, but she had taken Cressida's hand one day and made a long speech which Cressida couldn't understand, and then shaken it vigorously. Friends for life, thought Cressida happily. She did her best not to think about Aldrik and as the days went by she decided sadly that she wouldn't see him again. He had come into her life and gone again and there was nothing to do about it.

She went to see Charity on her first free day; the baby was expected any day now and that was all they talked about. There was a nurse already in the house and the children were wildly excited. Tyco came home while she was there and Cressida felt a pang of envy at the tender care he gave his wife. To be loved like that...

Aldrik hadn't been mentioned and when she could bear it no longer she asked how he was in what she hoped was a casual manner.

'Aldrik?' said Charity, 'Oh, he's in Brazil—or do I mean Argentina?—on a lecture tour. He won't be back for a bit. He said he's going to be back in time for the christening, though.' Charity sneaked a quick look at Cressida. 'That was lucky that he went to the ter Beemstras' and found you. Were you scared?'

'Terrified, but it was Anna who had the worst of it, and Baby...'

'Anna shouldn't have taken her out,' said Charity in such a severe and matronly voice that Cressida laughed and Charity laughed with her.

It was at dinner that evening, sitting between the Beemstras, that Cressida found herself listening to their talk. From time to time they excused themselves and spoke their own language and she hadn't minded this, but now she understood some of what they were saying.

'She is not good enough for him,' declared the lady of the house, and, since Dutch, when correctly and not too quickly spoken, was at times understandable, Cressida understood that. 'But of course he is a rich man and well thought of and she can be charming. They are to marry soon, I hear.'

She smiled across the table at Cressida. 'Forgive us, we gossip, Cressida. We talk of Nicola van Germert, who is to marry very soon. I for one am sorry for her husband,' she added maddeningly, 'but let us talk of something else—how is Charity? They hope for a boy, I expect?'

Cressida said that yes, she thought they did, but since Charity had declared her intention of having at least four children it didn't matter much either way. A remark which was approved by Mevrouw ter Beemstra, being the proud mother of six.

Cressida lay awake for a good deal of the night. She wished that she understood the Dutch language so that she could find out about Nicola, she wished that she had the courage to ask whom she was to marry and above all she wished very much that Aldrik would come home again. If he was going to marry Nicola then she wanted to see him just once more. She went to sleep eventually and woke with a terrible headache. Love, she reflected, was by no means all it was cracked up to be.

CHAPTER NINE

DURING the next few days Cressida pondered the problem of finding out about Nicola and Aldrik—for of course it would be he—hadn't Mevrouw ter Beemstra described him even if she hadn't given him a name? Too good for Nicola, she had said, and rich. She supposed that to live in a house like his at Janslum as well as having another house at Leiden one would need to be rich... To ask outright was impossible, inviting a polite snub or at best arousing curiosity. She decided finally to wait until she saw Charity again.

On the evening before her day off Tyco phoned; Charity had had a son that morning. She could hear the pride and happiness in his voice as he told her. 'And I'm coming for you as we arranged in the morning,' he went on. 'Charity is splendidly fit and wants to see you. She can't wait to let you see little Tyco. Stay for lunch and help me keep the girls in order, they are so excited. Now could you get hold of Beatrix? I had better tell her the news.'

So Cressida spent her day admiring the baby and listening to a blissfully happy Charity, lying back on the day bed in the bedroom, wrapped in the prettiest gown Cressida had ever seen, and then going downstairs to keep the girls entertained while Tyco sat with his wife. The rooms were awash with flowers too and the phone rang all day so that by the evening Cressida was tired but awash too with the contented happiness all around her.

'I don't know what we should have done without you,' said Tyco, driving her back after tea. 'It hasn't been much of a day off for you.'

'I've loved it,' said Cressida, and she meant it. 'And Charity looks lovely—it must be so nice to have a baby in your home and not in a hospital ward.'

Tyco chuckled. 'Ah, that is one of the advantages of marrying into the medical profession.'

It was long afterwards as she got ready for bed that she wished that she had been quick enough to ask about Aldrik and Nicola; it would have been easy to say, 'Oh, by the way, talking about doctors, how is Aldrik?'

'I'll never know,' she muttered unhappily, 'for there is no one to tell me.'

Someone did tell her, however, the very next day.

She had come indoors with the three girls after a brisk walk and was on her way upstairs to the playroom where Anna would be waiting in her chair to keep an eye on them for an hour while Cressida had some time to herself, when Mevrouw ter Beemstra came out of the drawing-room.

'Cressida, you have a caller, will you come down as soon as you have seen to the children?'

She had smiled but she had looked put out too and Cressida wondered why. Who on earth would want to see her? If it had been Tyco she would have been told at once and surely it wasn't Aldrik? Her heart leapt at the thought. It seemed to her that it took longer than usual to get the children's outdoor things off and tidied away and to make sure that they had all they needed to amuse them for an hour, and Anna wanted to talk— Cressida was too kind-hearted to cut her short. By the time she had tidied her hair and done something to her face fifteen minutes had gone by. She hoped the caller, whoever he or she was, wasn't impatient. It was on the way downstairs that she remembered the *domine*. She was smiling as she opened the drawing-room door.

Nicola was sitting, very much at her ease, in one of the armchairs by the fire, and Mevrouw ter Beemstra, sitting opposite her, turned round as Cressida paused in the doorway.

'There you are, Cressida. Nicola has been staying up here and thought she would call and see how you are getting on. I'll leave you to have a talk—you'll stay for a cup of tea?' she asked Nicola.

'No, no—I must get back—there is so much to do. I know you will forgive me.'

Mevrouw ter Beemstra looked relieved as she went away.

Nicola glanced around the room. 'How fortunate that you are so well settled here. The children are still young too, so you can depend on staying for a long time yet. It is such a relief to us.'

'Us?' Cressida asked quietly.

'Well, Aldrik and myself, of course. Who else? We have been concerned about you...'

'How kind. When are you getting married?'

Nicola looked down at her lap, hiding the gleam of triumph in her eyes; someone must have misled Cressida into thinking that she was marrying Aldrik. Well, she for one wasn't going to enlighten her; she had come to make mischief but there was no need. Let the silly girl go on believing that Aldrik and she were to marry—serve her right. She didn't want Aldrik herself now; she had been furious when he had made it plain to her that any idea of marrying her had been something she had thought up for herself without encouragement from him, as indeed it had been. Her pride not her heart had been hurt, for she had every intention of marrying a man she had known for some time, a man with a great deal of money and the lifestyle she enjoyed. It had rankled though that Aldrik had refused to dance to her tune and she at once saw a chance to get even with him and mislead the plain creature sitting opposite to her.

She said sweetly, 'Very soon.' She smiled and twisted the diamond ring on her finger and Cressida said,

'When he comes back from his lecture tour?'

'The very next day,' agreed Nicola, busy thinking up plausible lies. 'He asked me to come and see you—he had some silly idea that you had begun to like him a little too much.'

She watched the colour come into Cressida's cheeks and hid a smile. 'Of course I told him that was nonsense, I mean you haven't anything in common, have you?'

Cressida didn't answer that. Instead she said steadily, 'I hope you will be very happy. Janslum is such a lovely home...'

'Janslum? I hate the place.' Nicola saw Cressida's surprised look and hastily amended that. 'I love his home in Leiden and after all he works there for most of the time. He travels too from time to time and of course I shall go with him.'

Cressida asked politely, 'I expect you know Lady Merrill?'

Nicola knew her; on the one occasion when Lady Merrill had gone over to Janslum they had met and felt a mutual antipathy for each other. 'Such a charming old lady, we got on splendidly,' she said smugly.

She was clever enough to leave it at that. 'Well I must be on my way. Aldrik will wonder where I've got to—

he phones each evening, luckily Janslum isn't all that distance and the roads are almost clear again.'

Cressida got up. 'I'll fetch Mevrouw ter Beemstra, you will want to say goodbye...'

'No, no, don't disturb her. She knew that I had come to see you.'

Cressida accompanied her to the door, her feelings at boiling-point behind the polite emptiness of her unassuming features. She wished Nicola goodbye, waited until she had got into her car and driven away and then relieved her feelings by putting out a tongue in a childish gesture.

'I did not know that you were a friend of Nicola's,' observed Mevrouw ter Beemstra later that day.

'I'm not, *Mevrouw*. She only came to see me because someone had asked her to.'

'I do not care for her. She does not like children,' said Mevrouw ter Beemstra darkly.

'I don't like her either,' agreed Cressida, and went to the playroom to help the boys with their English lesson.

It wasn't until she was in her room getting ready for bed that she had the time to think about her own affairs. She went over Nicola's news, trying to remember every word that she had said. She hadn't said exactly when Aldrik was returning but she had given the strong impression that it was soon. Her cheeks grew hot, remembering what Nicola had said—that he was afraid that she had grown to like him too much. She couldn't and she wouldn't see him again, she had mistaken pity for friendship and liking and that tasted bitter in her mouth. Somehow she would have to go back to England. That was easier said than done; in fact, she couldn't think how it would be possible. The ter Beemstras had been so kind to her, paid her well and treated her as one of themselves, and she was very grateful. To leave them was unthinkable—more than that, impossible.

She was sitting with the twins on the following morning, patiently showing them a large map of the world and reciting the countries in English, when their mother came into the room.

'Cressida, I would like to talk—if Sepke and Galske could amuse themselves for a while?'

'I'll get their painting books. Would you like me to come downstairs?'

'Please.' She went away, leaving Cressida wondering what they would have to talk about—the little girls going to school, she supposed, or perhaps the boys weren't doing as well with their English at school as their father expected. She fetched paints and water and painting books, told them to be good children and ran downstairs.

Mevrouw ter Beemstra was in the drawing-room, a half-knitted pullover for one of the boys in her lap. 'Come and sit down, Cressida,' she said kindly. 'While you were out with the children there was a telephone call for you—a Miss Mogford. She wished to speak to you urgently. I told her that you would be back shortly and she asked that you should ring her after half-past eleven...'

'Moggy,' exclaimed Cressida, 'but she's not on the phone—she was our housekeeper before my father died—she's retired now.'

'She was telephoning from a—a box. Is that right? Therefore she tells me the time that you should ring her. It is a quarter past eleven now. When it is time, go to the library, it is quiet there, and see what is the matter. I hope it is not bad news...'

'Was she—did she sound upset?'

'Crying, I believe. I had a little difficulty understanding her...'

'Well, she's a Dorset woman, and she doesn't speak in the same way as someone from London or one of the big cities.'

'I understand. Like our Anna. You are fond of her, Cressida?'

'She came to my mother and father when they married, so I've known her all my life.' The remembrance of Moggy's elderly face brought a lump into Cressida's throat. 'I'm very fond of her.'

'We will have a cup of coffee together and then it will be time to telephone,' said Mevrouw ter Beemstra, 'and if it is necessary then you must go to your home and give her what help is needed. I hope that will not be so, but if it is then we will help you.'

Cressida thanked her, put down her coffee-cup and went to the library, the one room in the house where the children were not allowed to enter unless they were invited by their father. She dialled the number Mevrouw ter Beemstra had taken down. A moment later she heard Moggy's soft Dorset voice.

'Miss Cressy? I'm that sorry to bother you but I don't know what to do. I'm at my wits' end and no one to ask. It's all so sudden like and I'm sure my sister never meant it...'

'Moggy, dear, it's all right,' Cressida spoke encouragingly. 'Just tell me what has happened and I'll help. Is your sister ill?'

'She's dead. Oh, Miss Cressy whatever shall I do? She meant to alter her will, see, and leave the cottage to me, but she died sudden like and it's to go to her husband's nephew and 'e says as I must be out by the end of the month, and there's 'er two cats and he don't want 'em, and who's to take in two cats? For I'll not leave them...'

'The end of the month. That's two weeks away. Moggy, I'm coming back—I'll see the solicitors for you and see what can be done. Now don't worry, Mevrouw ter Beemstra has said that I can go to England if I'm needed. I'll be with you in a few days. Just stay where you are, Moggy. Don't sign anything and if anyone bothers you just say that I'll deal with them when I get there.'

'But your job, Miss Cressy——'

'I'm sure that I can come back, Moggy.' As she spoke Cressida realised that here was the chance she had wanted to leave Friesland, to go as far away from Aldrik as she could. It was strange that now that she had it she was loath to take it. All her good resolutions dissolved before her longing to see Aldrik just once more. Only for a moment; then Moggy's voice interrupted her thoughts.

'You will come, Miss Cressy?'

'Yes, Moggy. Just as soon as I can—two or three days...'

She said goodbye and went to tell Mevrouw ter Beemstra about it.

'Of course you must go, Cressida. A seat will be booked on a plane for you and we will drive to Schiphol with you and you are to stay as long as it is necessary. We will miss you very much, but it is your duty. You wish to go at once?'

'I explained to Miss Mogford that I would try and get to her in two or three days' time and she is content with that. Could I go the day after tomorrow? I can talk to Anna and explain to the children and pack, and please may I phone Charity?'

'Better than that, you shall definitely go and see her. Tomorrow morning Sepke and Galske are to spend an hour or two at the school they will go to next term. Anna can look after Baby, the boys will not be here, so you will be free. Take the little car and go over to the van der Bronses'.'

'You're so kind,' said Cressida soberly, 'and I'm leaving you in the lurch.'

'Lurch? What is this lurch?' and when Cressida explained she said, 'Think not of lurches,' and she added magnanimously 'We are in your debt. All shall be arranged.'

Charity was in the nursery, where Cressida had expected her to be. She had driven herself over in the little Mini and Jolly admitted her and ushered her without ceremony upstairs.

Charity was on a low stool dressing her infant son, but she looked up with real pleasure when she saw Cressida.

'How nice—you're just in time for coffee.' She did up poppers with brisk efficiency, kissed the feathery hair on the small head and popped her son into his cot. 'Nanny is in the next room...' She stood for a moment while a cosily plump person in a white apron came into the room and settled by the window with her knitting and then she took Cressida's arm.

Downstairs in the small sitting-room at the back of the house she said, 'You never come like this—suddenly—what's happened, Cressy?'

Over coffee Cressida told her. 'So I'll have to go back to Templecombe,' she finished, 'but I'm not sure if I shall be able to come back.'

'Do you want to?' asked Charity. 'There's some other reason, isn't there? I won't pry.' She busied herself filling

up their cups. 'Did you see Nicola when she came?
Heaven knows why she needed to call and congratulate
us; she couldn't care less. I was surprised that she was
going to see the ter Beemstras—they hardly know each
other.'

'She came to see me.'

Charity handed the biscuits and waited.

'She's going to be married. She came to tell me, she
said that—that Aldrik had asked her to see me.'

'He's not even in Holland.'

'No, but he's coming back quite soon, they're going
to be married as soon as he's home. I—I want to go
before he gets here.' Cressida lifted her unhappy gaze to
her friend's face. 'She said that he had sent her because
he was afraid that I was getting too fond of him.'

'Are you, Cressy?'

'Oh, yes, only I didn't think that it showed. I've been
so careful—only I thought that we were friends. I feel
so silly, I can't possibly meet him again. I was wondering what I should do and then Moggy phoned.'

'I don't believe that they are going to be married,'
said Charity. 'In fact...' She didn't go on; she could be
wrong, for she hadn't had much interest in any world
but her own happy one for the last few days. Tyco might
know and if he didn't he would find out and tell her
what to do. 'Ah,' she asked instead, 'and when do you
plan to go?'

'Tomorrow. Mijnheer ter Beemstra is driving me to
Schiphol. They've been very kind. I shall be in
Templecombe by the evening.'

'Have you enough money?'

'Yes, thank you. They're paying my fare. If I don't
come back I must return it.'

'Don't do that, Cressy; they want to repay you for all you've done and for going out to look for Anna and Baby.' She hesitated. 'Is there anything I can do for you—messages or the like?'

Cressida got to her feet. 'No, Charity, dear, I'll say my goodbyes tomorrow but please say goodbye to Tyco for me and thank you both for being so kind to me. I've been very happy here. I'm glad I was here when little Tyco was born. Oh, and I do love the little girls.'

Charity went to the door with her and watched her get into the Mini. Tyco was in Leeuwarden at the hospital, it would be easy enough to ring him up, but he would be home at teatime and he would know what to do. She waved goodbye and went indoors, longing for the day to be over and for Tyco's reassuring calm.

There was one other person Cressida wanted to say goodbye to—the *domine*. He was in his study at the severe little house by the church, writing what she supposed was his sermon. He was pleased to see her but his face fell when she told him why she had come.

'I had hoped that you would be staying with us,' he told her. 'I believe that we might have become good friends.'

'Well, I hope we're friends already,' said Cressida, 'I've been very happy here, you know and I'll not forget any of you. Perhaps we shall meet again one day.'

'You do not intend to come back?'

'I don't know. It very much depends on Miss Mogford. I can't just leave her, you see—she was with my family for years and years and she has no family now that her sister has died, and no money.'

'That is sad. You will miss us, then?'

'Indeed I shall.'

'But I think that there is some reason why you wish to go away from Friesland and not return.' His eyes searched her face. 'You do not wish to talk about it but I would respect your confidence.'

'Oh, I know you would, and you're quite right, there is a reason I want to go away from here. If Miss Mogford hadn't telephoned me I think that I would have gone anyway; the only thing that would have stopped me was the inconvenience to Mevrouw ter Beemstra.'

Presently she said goodbye and drove back to the house, packed her case and went to talk to Anna in the queer mixture of Dutch and English which they used together, and then when Mevrouw ter Beemstra came back with the twins there were the careful explanations to make the little girls understand and the last-minute arrangements to make with their mother.

Leave-taking was hard; she hadn't realised quite how much she had absorbed of the life in Friesland and now that she was going away she felt that she was leaving part of herself behind. She had been happy there and she had grown to love Aldrik there too; it wasn't just part of herself, she reflected sadly, it was her whole heart. Since there was nothing else to be done, however, she would do her best to forget him and make a new life in England. She would have to help Moggy first, of course, although she had no idea at the moment how she could. She would at least go and see Mr Tims or write to him and get his advice. If the nephew who was to have the house didn't want to live in it he might even agree to rent it to her at a rent she could afford; he might even be generous enough to add a little to her pension and if she could herself find a job locally she could get settled in the house with Moggy and share the expenses. It would be like old times ...

She watched the flat coast of Holland disappear under the plane's wing, fighting her tears. Everyone had been so kind; the children had been upset and so had the ter Beemstras and she was really going to miss Charity and Tyco.

She swallowed her tears with the coffee and then concentrated on the problem of settling poor Moggy.

She was in Templecombe by teatime. The cottage was close to the station and she walked to it, burdened by her heavy case and a plastic bag filled with presents from the children and several packages from Charity and Mevrouw ter Beemstra, as well as the rather wilted bunch of flowers she had bought at Schiphol for Moggy; she had bought a bottle of wine too. It might help them to make sensible plans together.

Moggy, she saw with a shock, had aged in the few months since they had last seen each other, but her welcome was very warm.

Moggy, who never cried, cried now. 'I'm a selfish old woman,' she mumbled into Cressida's sympathetic shoulder, 'but I'm at my wits' end. A couple of weeks, that's all I've got to find somewhere to go. I went along to the job centre in Yeovil but the lady there said I'd find it difficult to get anything—I'm too old.'

'Hush, Moggy, dear,' said Cressida, 'I'm going to write to Mr Tims and see if he can help and if he can't I'll go and see Stepmother and ask her to help. Then I'll get a job and we can pay her back. I'd better see whoever is advising the nephew...'

'It's Snide and Snide in Yeovil—my sister's nephew lives in Leeds.'

They had dropped everything in the little hall and gone to sit in the kitchen and Moggy had made tea.

'You mean to say that he is coming here to live?'

Moggy shook her head. 'That's just it—he's going to sell the place lock, stock and barrel—there's been one or two enquiries already.'

'Is he a poor man?'

Moggy snorted. 'Got a tidy little business, 'e 'as, no children and a wife who goes out to work.'

Cressida finished her tea. 'Well, you're not to worry any more, Moggy. I'm sure something can be done about it.'

She spoke reassuringly, but she had her doubts, and Moggy was too upset to share them.

She went first to Snide and Snide where, after being kept waiting for all of half an hour, she was seen by the junior partner in the firm, a young man who took one look at her and decided that this rather plain girl with the quiet voice hardly merited his full attention. No, he told her, their client was adamant about Miss Mogford leaving the cottage; he intended to sell it.

'How much does he want for it?' asked Cressida.

He named a sum which she thought excessive, and in any case there was no hope in raising such a sum unless her stepmother would help.

She went away presently and was glad to go. She didn't like the younger Mr Snide and she was aware that he felt the same about her. She tried Mr Tims next, this time with a carefully worded letter, and she received a reply by return of post telling her that really there was little he could do unless she was in a position to buy the cottage. However, he did promise to look into the matter in case there was some loophole.

Cressida was discouraged but she had no intention of giving up. Despite protests from Moggy she took herself off to her home.

The girl who answered the door knew Cressida. 'Miss Cressida—have you come back home? How nice to see you...'

'I've only come to see my stepmother, Mary. If you would tell her I'm here, please?'

Her stepmother looked up from her chair as she went in.

'Cressida—the last person I expected to see. Why have you come? You didn't expect to be welcome, did you?'

'No. I wouldn't have come on my own account. I want to talk to you about Miss Mogford.' Cressida sat down unbidden. 'If you would listen,' she began, and explained briefly. 'I wondered if you would lend us the money to buy the cottage? I'll pay you back as soon as I've got a job; something each month.'

Her stepmother gave an angry laugh. 'What a silly little fool you are, Cressida. Do you really suppose that I would lift a finger to help either you or Miss Mogford? You've wasted money on a bus, my girl. Now go away and don't come back; next time you won't be admitted.'

There was nothing for it but to go back to Moggy, to make light of her visit to her stepmother and tell her that there was almost a fortnight still, 'And anything could happen,' said Cressida hearteningly. A statement which seemed to cheer Moggy but which did nothing to improve her own low spirits.

Three days after Cressida had gone back to England the doctor returned to Holland. His lecture tour had been successful, even if gruelling, and he had carried out his role as examiner of medical students in several of the medical schools he had visited with such proficiency that he had earned high praise. He had no thought for that. On the long flight back he bent his powerful brain to the ways and means of seeing Cressida as soon as possible. She had got under his skin and taken possession of his heart as well and he supposed with hindsight that he had fallen in love with her the moment he had set eyes on her, sitting forlornly on the grass with Caesar. She was, he reflected, the only woman in the world for him; he would tell her so the moment he saw her. Before then he had commitments which couldn't be ignored; by the time the plane landed at Schiphol he had a tightly scheduled programme planned which he had whittled down to three days' hard work in Leiden. Far too long but she would still be there...

Wester was waiting for him with the Bentley, the two dogs in the back, panting with delight at the sight of him, and they drove at once to Leiden. It was still early morning and the doctor, stopping only to shower and eat his breakfast, went to the hospital to confer with his registrar, see his patients and in the afternoon take an out-patients clinic.

'You're doing too much, Doctor,' said Wester severely when he got back to his house, and Mies chimed in,

'All that way in one of those dreadful aeroplanes, too, you're tired to the bone and don't deny it.'

The doctor looked from one to the other of his faithful old friends. 'Yes, I'm tired, but I want to get to Janslum as soon as I can and that means doing some work.'

He didn't say why he needed to go but they both nodded and when he had gone to his study Mies said, 'It'll be that nice English miss he brought here...'

Wester nodded. 'He brought her to Janslum, a *deftig* young lady.'

It was midnight of the third day when the doctor opened his house door content that he had done everything he had planned to do. Now he was free to go to

Friesland. Too late tonight, he reflected, but first thing in the morning...

He and Wester and the dogs set off before it was light, sent on their way by a cosily wrapped Mies. Halfway there, he said, 'Phone Tyske, will you, Wester, and ask her to have breakfast for us—in about an hour's time?'

It was a cold morning, inclined to drizzle from a low-ering sky, and it was no better by the time they had breakfasted. The doctor took the dogs for a brisk walk and then got into his car and drove rather too fast to the ter Beemstras' house. It was mid morning now and he judged that Cressida would be available.

It was Beatrix ter Beemstra who came to greet him when he was admitted. 'How nice to see you, have you had a good trip? You have been away for too long—were the lectures successful?'

Aldrik was a man of monumental patience; he even spent several minutes discussing the weather, enquiring after the children and Anna's leg before asking to see Cressida.

'She's not here—you didn't know? No, of course you didn't. She went back to England six days ago. Her old housekeeper telephoned—she was in some kind of trouble and Cressida said that she would have to go and help her.' Beatrix glanced at the deceptively calm face before her. 'I think she was glad to go—indeed, she said that she needed to get away. She didn't say why and I didn't ask her. She is a dear girl and she would not have wished that unless her reasons were very real.'

'You have her address?'

'Well, I'm afraid not—when she went she went within a day, you know, and there was so much to arrange. Charity will know, however. We miss her very much—such a gentle girl.'

The doctor stayed for a few minutes longer, making polite small talk, and then he got into the Bentley again and drove to Charity's house.

Here he had no need to stand on ceremony. He gave her a friendly hug and she kissed his cheek and then stood back to look at him.

'Before I take you to see your godson, Aldrik, Cressy's either with this Miss Mogford or at her stepmother's. I'll tell you about it and you'll know what to do. Please come and see the infant Tyco first, then we'll have coffee and I'll tell you as much as I know.'

The baby was asleep. Charity hung over the cot. 'The spitting image of his dad,' she said proudly. 'Next time when you come perhaps he'll be awake.'

'He's a splendid fellow and you are right, he is just like Tyco. Do the girls like him?'

'When they are at home I have to fight my way to get at him—we're all so happy...' She stopped and went pink. 'And you're not, are you? But you will be. Come downstairs and we'll talk.'

Over coffee she explained about Nicola's visit. 'I knew it wasn't true but she had made it all seem as though it were and it was unforgivable of her to tell Cressy those lies about you being afraid that she was getting fond of you. No wonder she couldn't wait to get back to England. Poor old Miss Mogford's troubles came at just the right time.'

She peeped at Aldrik's face. It looked quite frighteningly grim.

'I can catch the night ferry,' he said at once, 'and be there during the morning. Have you Miss Mogford's address?'

'Yes, I've written it down for you, but she may be at her stepmother's house. I'd go there first. Will you go to Lady Merrill's?'

He nodded. 'I can call in at Cressy's home on the way.' He got to his feet, 'My dear, you've been a real friend.' He bent to kiss her. 'Tell Tyco I'll see him when we get back and be sure and take care of that son of yours.'

When he got back home he told Wester to pack a bag and book a berth on the night ferry from the Hoek and then he took the dogs for a long walk. The time had to be filled in before he could leave for England.

He drove away from Harwich on a dismal grey morning, he had had breakfast on board and he didn't intend to stop until he reached Cressy's home, he had studied the map and took the road through Hatfield, Watford and Slough, cutting out London entirely, to join the M3 and later on the A303. He drove steadily, keeping to the maximum speed, and the further west he went, the better the weather. When at last he stopped in the drive before Cressida's home the sun was shining.

Mrs Preece was coming downstairs as the maid admitted him. She recognised him at once and came forward, smiling archly. 'Doctor—how delightful to see you again. You are on your way to see Lady Merrill? Too late for coffee, but do have a drink and tell me all your news.'

'You are very kind, but I can't stop. I came to see if Cressida is here?'

The smile became fixed. 'Certainly not. She walked out of this house and she can stay out of it.'

'But has she been here recently?'

'Why do you want to know?' and when he didn't answer, and just stood there looking at her, she said,

'She came here two days ago, if you must know.' She added sulkily, 'She wanted to borrow money to buy Miss Mogford's sister's cottage, if you please. I sent her packing.'

'Back to Miss Mogford's?' The doctor's voice was very quiet.

'How should I know? The old woman's got all she deserves anyway, leaving me in the lurch—it's impossible to get servants nowadays.'

'I'm sorry to have disturbed your morning,' said Aldrik smoothly and bade her goodbye. His poor little Cressida, he thought, getting into his car and taking the road to his grandmother's house. While he had been with Mrs Preece he had been thinking; contacting Mr Tims might be the best thing to do. It wasn't much use seeing Cressida unless he knew exactly how matters stood.

Lady Merrill was delighted to see him. 'Lunch,' she told him briskly, 'you're worn out. Why are you here? Something to do with Cressida, I'll be bound.'

He told her over lunch. 'I think I'd better get hold of Tims,' he finished, 'now.'

Mr Tims made everything plain in a few as dry-as-dust sentences.

'Can I buy the place?' asked the doctor. 'Will this man sell?'

'If the price is attractive, yes.'

'Will you phone him, ask him what price he wants, and buy it?'

Mr Tims was shocked. 'My dear Aldrik, aren't you being a bit hasty? A little bargaining...'

'Will you hasten and phone him now and ring me back?—I'll be here for the next hour or so.'

'Very well. You're throwing money away...'

Mr Tims hung up and began to dial another number. He had always been impressed by Aldrik's calm manner and good sense but he had sounded very unlike himself. Half an hour later he phoned Lady Merrill's house.

'Well, you have your cottage,' he told the doctor, 'and you've paid double its worth.' He sounded faintly disapproving but Aldrik took no notice. 'Splendid, and thank you—now there's one thing more...' He began to speak and Mr Tims, listening, permitted himself a smile.

Cressida was putting on the kettle for a cup of tea—Moggy liked her tea sharp at four o'clock—when the knocker was thumped and a small boy handed her an envelope. It was addressed to her and she turned it over in a useless sort of way while he waited. His fidgeting roused her, though; she found her purse and gave him twenty pence and went back to the kitchen where she opened it. It was from Mr Tims asking her to go to the office; if she would go to Brown's Garage a car would take her. He would expect her within the next half hour.

Cressida read it twice, roused Moggy from her nap and read it to her and then went to get her outdoor things. 'That nephew of your sister's has changed his mind,' she declared. 'I dare say he's at Mr Tims's office now. But I wonder why it's just me he wants?'

'I dare say you'll understand what's being said better than me,' said Moggy. 'Don't you waste a moment, Miss Cressy; 'e'd never 'ave a taxi for you if it weren't important.'

Mr Tims's office was in a side-street, its windows discreetly curtained and the doorknocker splendidly polished. Cressida beat a tattoo on it and was admitted by a clerk and told to go upstairs to Mr Tims's room.

Outside the door she took a deep breath and knocked, and, requested to enter, did so.

Mr Tims was sitting behind his desk and the doctor was lounging against the window, his large person obscuring most of the light of a fading day.

'Oh,' said Cressida inadequately, but since she had lost her breath for a moment it would have to do.

'Hello, Cressy,' said the doctor in a voice of such tenderness that she lost her breath again, which gave Mr Tims the chance to speak.

'I have asked you to come here at Dr van der Linus's request. He has purchased the cottage in which Miss Mogford is at present living so that she may stay there for the rest of her life.'

He glanced up. Neither of the two people with him were listening, or so it seemed to him, they were looking at each other in a manner which suggested that they were unaware of him, or anything else for that matter.

'The doctor will explain,' he said in his dry voice, and went out of the room.

'I'll explain later,' said Aldrik and crossed the room in two strides to wrap Cressy in his great arms, 'and we'll have no more of this, you'll marry me so that I know where you are and what you are doing. You've been disrupting my whole life—I have never met such a girl.'

He kissed her very hard and then again, gently this time. 'My darling tiresome girl, I love you.' He smiled down at her. 'Will you marry me?'

She smiled, her ordinary face suddenly beautiful. 'Well, yes, I should like that very much, but first shouldn't you explain?'

'A waste of time,' said the doctor testily, 'there are other things more important.'

'If you say so, dear Aldrik.' She sounded meek but her eyes sparkled.

The doctor studied her face with great satisfaction. 'My beautiful girl,' he said, and fell to kissing her once more.

It was nice to be called beautiful, reflected Cressida, kissing him back with goodwill, even though it wasn't true, and, anyway, she felt beautiful. With what breath she had left she said, 'Aldrik...'

'"For God's sake hold your tongue, and let me love",' growled the doctor, and meant every word; John Donne's age-old plea seemed exactly right for the occasion.

Let
HARLEQUIN ROMANCE®
take you

BACK TO THE RANCH

Come to the Lucky Horseshoe Ranch, near Pepper, Texas!

Meet Cody Bailman—cattle rancher, single father and Texan—and Sherry Waterman, a nurse-midwife who's new to town.

Read LONE STAR LOVIN' by Debbie Macomber, July's Back to the Ranch title!

Available wherever Harlequin Books are sold.

RANCH2

New York Times Bestselling Author

Sandra Brown

Tomorrow's Promise

**She cherished the memory
of love but was consumed
by a new passion too
fierce to ignore.**

For Keely Preston, the memory of her husband
Mark has been frozen in time since the day he was
listed as missing in action. And now, twelve years
later, twenty-six men listed as MIA have been
found.

Keely's torn between hope for Mark and despair
for herself. Because now, after all the years of
waiting, she has met another man!

**Don't miss TOMORROW'S PROMISE by
SANDRA BROWN.**

**Available in June wherever Harlequin
books are sold.**